I0561338

DEEP AIR

ABSOLUTELY AMA ING eBOOKS

Habent Sua Fata Libelli

ABSOLUTELY AMAZING eBOOKS

Manhanset House
Shelter Island Hts., New York 11965-0342

bricktower@aol.com • tech@absolutelyamazingebooks.com
• absolutelyamazingebooks.com

All rights reserved under the International and Pan-American Copyright Conventions. No part of this publication may be reproduced, stored in a retrieval system, or transmitted in any form or by any means, electronic, or otherwise, without the prior written permission of the copyright holder. The Absolutely Amazing eBooks colophon is a trademark of J. T. Colby & Company, Inc.

Library of Congress Cataloging-in-Publication Data
Perkins, Reef
Deep air
p. cm.

1. FICTION / Humorous / Black Humor. 2. FICTION / Thrillers / Crime. 3. FICTION / Mashups
Fiction, I. Title.
ISBN: 978-1-955036-14-6, Trade Paper

Copyright © 2016 by Reef Perkins
Electronic compilation/ paperback edition
copyright © 2016 by Absolutely Amazing eBooks
Poem reprinted with the permission of Simon and Schuster, Inc. from *Generation Of Swine* by Hunter S. Thompson. Copyright © 1988 by Hunter S. Thompson. All rights reserved.

July 2022

DEEP AIR

Reef Perkins

ABSOLUTELY AMAZING eBOOKS

For Roberta

"It was the Law of the Sea, they said. Civilization ends at the waterline. Beyond that, we all enter the food chain, and not always right at the top."
— *Hunter S. Thompson*

"There is no dilemma compared with that of the deep-sea diver who hears the message from the ship above. 'Come up at once. We are sinking.' "
—Robert Cooper

You gotta go down, but you don't gotta come up

DEEP AIR

Sleek reef sharks jerked the still warm body into deeper water, down and away from a phantasmagoria of impassive eyes and snapping mouths, deep into the cold silent world of "Who's eating whom?"

Interested only in flesh, the swimming teeth spit out bits of clothing, shoes, condoms, chump change and a cheap wedding ring. The regurgitated token of forgotten promises landed on a piece of staghorn coral shaped like a middle finger and remains an undigested testimonial to an unpleasant man.

~ ~ ~

At the confluence of the Gulf of Mexico and the Atlantic Ocean, Gorton's Marina presents a carbuncle of termite-infested buildings nestled along the shore and shallow water of Key West Harbor, near old the shrimp docks and upwind of the Toxic Triangle.

Gorton's consists of a rotting marina building where a faded CLOSED sign has dangled for over twenty years. Further on, a combination outdoor shower and BBQ pit, crushed oyster shell parking lot, tilting Tiki huts and rotted wooden walkways lead to three floating docks, a floating bar called the *Fly Strip Lounge* and one unisex toilet, also floating.

The docks creak rhythmically to satisfy the tidal surge and the bobbing poop chute challenges visitors and locals alike. Those who seek "the bowl" on a blustery day amuse others who themselves struggle at the undulating bar like a row of boozed-up bobble heads.

1

~ ~ ~

Gorton's, a quiet place, a place where one can pour a drink down the front of ones shirt and no one will notice. A place where now becomes then, where here becomes there, a place where time turns inward to feed upon itself and the damp salt-sucking atmosphere encourages unusual sorts to grow, like mold.

Old timers say you can only find Gorton's if you're lost.

McCREEDY

Moored at the end of the main dock, the thirty-foot sailing vessel, *Faulty Dog,* bobbed patiently through sun and storm and waited for a new lover to arrive. She had not been to sea in twenty years and tugged at her lines like a flat-chested transvestite in a pirate bodice. She hoped her new lover, *if the asshole ever showed up,* would be more enthusiastic than the last nine losers. She only had X-number of good bobs left in her.

White as a marshmallow, sporting a Canadian flag T-shirt, mismatched flip flops and a lopsided mustache, a newcomer, Dick McCreedy, sought and bought the *Faulty Dog* from an old salt known as Fire Ant.

They met in the *Fly Strip Lounge* and after hearing Dick's story, Fire Ant took Dick on a short walk and quick tour of the *Faulty Dog.* McCreedy asked Fire Ant to start the engine. It worked. That's all Dick needed to know. McCreedy passed Fire Ant a wad of cash and they sealed the deal with a cold Key Deer beer at the *Fly Strip.*

After a few minutes of meaningless conversation, Fire Ant took a final gulp, crushed his beer can with one squeeze, stood up and gave Dick a similar grasp across the shrimp-scented table, "Don't sail her out, if you can't sail her in. Get my drift, son?"

Fire Ant thumbed his newly acquired wad, adjusted his shorts and ambled down the rickety rotten dock. He paused at the gift shop and decided to celebrate the sale with the purchase of a new hat.

"I want a good one," he told the clerk.

Fire Ant exited the shop. A small, lurking Latino laughed when a frightened gull took flight and jettisoned a load on Fire Ant's new straw hat.

The Ant paused, took a deep breath, one-fingered the laughing Latin and ambled on. He would leave his hat outside for a few days and let the tropic sun do its patient work. After all, there was no reason to be ornery; it was the third time he'd sold the *Dog* in the last twelve months.

Fire Ant stopped for a moment and stared at the Neptunal water. Lives are like boats, he thought, even bought and ready to go, some of them never leave the dock. Still, there's got to be some karma in there somewhere, right?

Dick waited until he got feeling back in his right hand then headed out to find a marine supply store. Four bags of ice, a cooler, one life jacket and two cases of Key Deer beer later he returned to the *Faulty Dog* and popped a cold one, guzzled and climbed below to nap.

An hour later, Dick awoke, went topsides, pumped his personal bilge, stole a bike and rode into town. He'd made a decent living committing insurance fraud in Canada but the arctic winters were getting colder and his cheating bill had gone up.

Dick found a marine insurance company on Mud Dauber Lane where, after fifteen minutes of sincere lying and inconclusive evidence, he managed to insure the *Faulty Dog* for thirty thousand dollars. He'd only paid Fire Ant five grand.

Back onboard the *Faulty Dog,* Dick popped another beer. *Phsssst!* The sound evoked a meditative state until a quick movement to his left caused him to turn. A flapping piece of paper was wedged in a crack near the companionway door. The words, "Time for dee Monies to be pay ..." were poorly penned on a receipt for a box of .22 caliber bullets. The note instructed him to meet a guy named Naldo in the parking lot behind the *Fly Strip Lounge* at ten o'clock the next morning. The note went on, "You will pay dee Monies or Dye or both." Dick ignored the spelling error and wondered if this missive was related to a recent venture during which he borrowed and lost fifteen thousand dollars on turtle races at the *South Florida Floppers* titty bar on Miami Beach. He fully intended to honor his commitment but it appears his low-life debtors tracked him down before he could make his move, eh.

Dick stuffed the note into his pocket and inhaled the fresh salt breeze. Finally, he sighed, sucked beer foam off his mustache, leaned back and *faux* meditated.

A deep-throated garfoon uttered forth as he dreamily wrenched his mustache even tighter, like a sailor pulling an anchor. The right side was much longer than the left from his habitual tugging and a pleasant, pain induced, smile gathered on his distended upper lip. It was, he knew, an unpleasant habit.

~ ~ ~

The next morning, a damp sun rose as Dick departed the *Faulty Dog,* walked up the dock, across the parking lot and sat in the shade of a tilting Tiki hut as instructed. He watched birds peck bugs on a nearby grave, opened a cold beer and waited for the stranger, Naldo, to arrive. The smell of fresh bait netted in the low water wafted across the picnic table. We're all bait, Dick thought and we all get caught when life gets too shallow. It made him sad. He slapped bugs, sipped booze and waited.

Meanwhile, a small tight-faced Latino arrived at the *Faulty Dog.*

Naldo Cone was dyslectic or vice-versa and forgot he was to meet McCreedy in the parking lot. Instead, he went back to where he'd left the note. Naldo was a simple-minded killer, a trail horse with a gun.

5

In a pocket over his heart, Naldo carried a ballistic bag containing four hundred faceted, blue-green emeralds. His boss, Senor Bonterra, a senior member of the brazen, Taco Blanco Cartel, intended to send the stones as payment for a load of cocaine from Columbia. But the Columbians, nervous about receiving the stones in the states, asked they be transferred offshore, in international waters. Bonterra was tasked with finding a boat and crew.

At the same time, a loan shark in Miami contracted Bonterra to find a fellow named Dick McCreedy. Senor Bonterra agreed to extract a payment of fifteen thousand dollars-plus five thousand dollars interest from Dick McCreedy, or kill him. During the phone call, Bonterra learned McCreedy's suspected location and sent his hit man, Naldo Cone the Enforcer, to find McCreedy.

~ ~ ~

Naldo carried an expensive Kevlar-lined, Key Deer skin, briefcase as he climbed onboard the *Faulty Dog* and banged on the companionway hatch. "*Hola, hola*, Deek?" No answer. "Where is deez fool McCreedy?" Naldo pushed the companionway hatch open and entered the cabin.

On the other side of the marina, under the tilting Tiki hut near the parking lot, Dick shook his head, "Where is that fool Naldo?" and opened another beer.

Both men were stupid. Both men were patient.

NALDO

Naldo sat in the hot, mildewed cabin. He practiced his sneer and uttered cruel, mispronounced threats that were his singular style in the enforcement business.

Around noon, Naldo tired of his vile dissertation. A true professional, he was easily bored and fully equipped. His was a lonely job, a job where the only ones who appreciated his work were dead.

He seized his hairy briefcase and moved quietly into the forward cabin, pushed mildewed sail bags aside and opened the case. His *amour globo*, his love balloon, his *Conchita,* sensuously unfolded from the confined space and he, just as quickly, morphed from Naldo Cone the Enforcer to Naldo Cone the Inflator and readied himself for *Conchita* who was, after all, the best of the inflatable, 4-ply, made in the USA, "Elastic Companions" on the market.

Naldo inserted a tropically scented nitrous oxide cartridge, pulled the strategically located ripcord and *voila,* he was not alone. Her slow expansion never failed to stir his pulled pork loins.

"I am a lonely hunter," he said to *Conchita's* rapidly inflating ass. *Conchita,* the classic *Tango Mucho Boom-Boom* model, came equipped with long dark plastic hair, an interchangeable "tropical" nipple kit and black mesh stockings designed for men with a used shrimp net fetish. *Conchita* spoke only poorly recorded Spanish. A high speed, low drag, six chambered, inflatable being-cum-life raft, her soft electronic voice purred when fully gassed up,

"*Buenos Dias, Senor,*" she cooed, "*Usted es mucho Grande, sí? Mucho Grande ... oooh, la, la ... Madre de la Carne.*"

While Naldo inflated his ego, a young man named Raul Mims stood silently on a nearby seawall.

Shorter than his shadow.

Mims, a small tightly-wound Latin wore an overcoat that touched the ground. He was shorter than his shadow and stood in the shade of a gumbo-limbo tree. The air was hotter than a habanero fart in a bucket seat.

Mims stared at the *Faulty Dog.* Although he had not actually seen his newest girlfriend, Babette, go onboard the boat, he knew the man who sto'-his-ho', lurked below.

Babette was easy fo'-a- ho' and Mims knew this after their first ten minute date. Still, knowing didn't ease the pain. He'd loved her as much as he loved the frilly white *guayabera* shirt his grandmother, Momo, made for his sixteenth birthday. Someone stole it off a dry cleaning rack in Hialeah and he felt now as he had then, disturbed.

"And now," Mims clenched his weak jaw, "this bad man Naldo must pay. Naldo, dee man who sto' my ho' with a promise that she would never have to give me a *mamada* again. *No es possible!*"

Mims learned of Naldo's alleged treachery weeks ago and, with the help of his father, Bad Mingo Mims, tracked Naldo from Miami to this dingy marina in Key West. Raul came to wreak traditional bloody revenge, a simple matter of pride, honor, a few bullets, one speeding ticket, a dozen conch fritters, four hemorrhoids, and a rental car.

Raul Mims twitched, one of his many drug induced afflictions and slapped at a mosquito. Being near-sighted, he often misjudged and hurt himself.

"*Conjo!* Get back on track Mims, it's time for the kill," he reminded himself. Mims had hunted small game all his life and knew this man, Naldo, would not be as fast as a Miami rat.

Without an obvious reason the *Faulty Dog* began bobbing rhythmically in the still water. Frayed dock lines squeaked from the seaborne pulsations. Mims ignored the somehow familiar motion and duct taped a custom silencer to the barrel of his revolver. He had made it himself from a Pillsbury Dough Boy cookie tube, untraceable.

Raul Mims boarded the *Faulty Dog*, slipped down the companionway into the dark cabin and found Naldo, pants around his ankles, vigorously humping in the forward cabin.

Ass-out, Naldo Cone didn't stand a chance and Mims wondered how Babette got onboard without being seen.

"*Naldo! Madre de Dios!* Is deez my sweet Babette," the near-sighted Mims cried in anguish. He pulled the silenced weapon out of his shorts and discharged five .22 rounds into the coupled bodies. The silencer exploded after the first round. Raul had forgotten to take the cookie dough out.

Babette, for her part, was in Delray Beach blowing a Nordic volleyball player and had never met Naldo.

Naldo turned to face his attacker and shielded the female form with his body. Mims fired bullet number six into Naldo's chest. Naldo gasped, fell backwards and landed on what Mims thought was Babette.

Even with the silencer there had been smoke, vulgar noises and a slight scent of baked goods. Mims fumbled forward in the dark, gun-smoke filled cabin and pushed sail bags over the bullet-ridden bodies. He'd never killed anything but rodents and time before and was surprised he had the balls to pop Naldo. "*Vaya con Carne, Babette,*" he muttered over his shoulder. He would not touch her nor bless her with his gaze. Mims had reclaimed his honor and never looked back.

He scuttled onto the dock and slipped into the shade to plan his escape just as the marina's automatic sprinkler system came on. "*Madre Dios!*"

Embraced by deathly calm waters, the *Faulty Dog* lay in a passionless tide, the dry hump induced ripples faded and white-foamed lips of vengeance lapped the shore. A dead grunt floated nearby, its bloated, milky eye followed Mims escape.

~ ~ ~

Gorton's Marina constructed in the 70's by local smugglers Morton and Norton Gorton, initially served as an unloading site for cocaine, sometimes called "nose food" or "Peruvian marching powder." After a few successes the brothers went straight, but remained unmarried. Neither could find anyone they loved more than themselves.

Dick waited and noticed two tilting crosses nearby. They were overgrown with flaming dingus weed and fashioned from broken fly rods and beer cans. While Dick ruminated on the spoor-specked markers of days gone by, a small dog paused and tilted to bless the site.

Suddenly hungry, Dick left the parking lot and walked toward the *Fly Strip Lounge*. He took a seat and ordered a fracked conch burger.

Nearby, Raul Mims fired up his rental car, put the top down and stomped on the gas. The neon blue Mustang convertible threw a pea rock rooster tail on customers' cars and headed north. "That's a buzz kill," one patron remarked.

McCreedy's single-minded grinding of the tasty gastropod was interrupted by this brutish display of poor driving skills, "What's the rush?" he mumbled and chewed.

Dick paid for lunch and continued to masticate his conch as he tottered toward the Tiki to wait, and continue chewing.

The conch is a tough character and proper chewing takes time and energy. Dick, a bi-molar Canadian, gnashed his teeth and shifted the conch cud back and forth in his mouth so his jaw wouldn't tire. He had to hold his mustache up to avoid ingesting it. It gave him something to do.

On the other hand, things were going good for Raul Mims until he hit a bull alligator at ninety-miles an hour, near Alabama Jack's on Card Sound road. With the top down and no properly fastened seat belt, Mims went airborne and followed by the bright blue Mustang, ungraciously plunged into the Everglades with a fast sucking sound. The bugs were bad. No one came to help, except the alligators.

Airborne at three, he was a turd by ten.

CONCHITA

In the forward cabin, Naldo, wounded but not dead, sniffed the warm nitrous oxide leaking from a bullet nick in *Conchita's* left buttock chamber. Naldo loved nitrous oxide. He often went to the dentist even if he didn't have a problem, just to get the gas. Naldo inhaled deeply and got a mild taste of nitrogen narcosis, the Rapture of the Deep, and for a moment the sweet gas made him question if there was more to life than killing people, but he couldn't figure out what it might be.

The gas wore off and like air squeaking through a stretched balloon neck, he heard the life fart out of his beloved. Naldo squeezed *Conchita,* (wrong thing to do,) tried to plug her wound with some Doughboy carcass and comforted himself with more nitrous oxide and a prayer.

Naldo bowed his head, "Stay with me my darling," he prayed, "stay with me. I don't know who the fuck that guy is but I pray he only winged you. That noisy, cheap-ass gun, man, he scared himself off. Dumb fuck didn't even check me for a pulse ... Amen."

With more holes than necessary in his ass, Naldo needed medical attention before he bled to death. Even in the confines of the cabin the shots had been loud enough to attract attention. The chance some do-good yachtsmen would report a man with a bleeding ass, dragging himself along the docks before lunch, were good. After a two-martini lunch, he'd stand a better chance of being ignored, but would bleed out by then.

It was time to go but his ribs hurt like he'd been punched. Naldo fingered his chicken chest and pulled the Kevlar pouch from his left shirt pocket. He'd forgotten about it and found a small hole in the pocket, a smaller hole in the pouch and no hole in his chest. Naldo looked at the sack and rubbed his bruised pectoral that looked like a perch filet. His eyes lit up, "*Madre Dios*-dee stones save me from making to die." He opened the bag and found a flattened .22 bullet among the frightened stones.

Before exiting the cabin, Naldo plugged the hole in the bag with some rapidly curing Doughboy and tucked the emeralds into *Conchita's* ample, intact and partially inflated Special Projects area. He pushed his landlubber rubber lover further into the forward cabin and pulled sail bags over her still hissing body. He hated to leave the stones but he looked bad and couldn't risk being stopped and searched.

"Wait for me, my *In-flat-tab-le.*" Naldo whispered and slunk away, like a scolded beagle.

Once ashore, Naldo stole a paper tablecloth from a nearby picnic table and fashioned a sarong to cover his hemorrhaging hiney. He didn't have the stones but, technically, they weren't lost. He knew where they were and intended to retrieve them; but first, Naldo needed a doctor and went to find *El Boss*.

~ ~ ~

Dick shook his head. It was three in the afternoon and Naldo remained a no- show. "Something is wrong. Five hours is too long to be late. Maybe they changed their minds and are going to try and whack me instead. I'll give him twenty minutes more, then, that's it, Plan B goes into action." Dick paused and stared at the doughnuts in the dirt left by the blue Mustang, they looked like the symbol for eternity.

After a few hours of chewing while sitting on warped pine boards, Dick's jaw hurt and butt was flatter than his beer. Thinking out loud, "Guess that Naldo ain't going to make it. Dang it! Its only fifteen grand I owe, but I coulda paid it all back. Oh well, who gives a rat's ass. Guess I'll hafta to keep all the money for my ownself, eh." Dick chuckled innocently at his lack of sincere guilt and guzzled the last of a warm one, got up and headed for the sailing vessel, *Faulty Dog*.

Although half in the bag and fore-sheets to the wind, Dick noticed a couple cops trundling up and down the docks, looking at boats.

He tucked into the bushes and waited.

One cop held a crackling radio to his ear as he walked past.

"Yeah, some bass-hole thought they heard shots around here somewhere, kinda smells like doughnuts, but I don't see shit .... Fuck! Over."

Dick clamped his hands over his lips to stifle gut-wrenching laughter and waited, waited until the cop scraped the offending dog turd off his shoe and moved on to find a hose.

After a few minutes, Dick boarded the *Faulty Dog* and glanced into the dark cabin. His survival bag and cooler were still on the cabin floor below. He thought he smelled fresh baked goods, "That's weird," he remarked, "maybe I'm drinking too much."

Without further preparation, Dick fired up the ancient diesel and opened a beer. Plan B was on the burner.

A HOLE IN THE WATER

In water flatter than day old road kill, the *Faulty Dog* slipped her sunburned lines and headed for sea. Her rubber dinghy trailed behind like a fat gray dog and came equipped with an outboard motor and a hand-held VHF radio. In the forward cabin, covered by sail bags, the wounded *Conchita* remained injured, butt unnoticed.

The shadows grew longer and two hours later, Dick crossed over Blinky's Hump, just north of Skinny Mon Key. The always-hungry Gulf Stream lay ahead.

Dick motored across the reef and checked his Fathometer, even though it didn't work. He scanned the horizon for vessels that might foil his plan or plot his position. Dick reached down the companionway and hoisted the backpack and cooler up on deck. He wished he'd remembered to buy a compass and motored on.

After three *beer-miles*, the sun dropped into the horizon like a flaming billiard ball in a cool blue pocket. Darkness ate the light.

Behind the *Dog's* curling wake a trail of phosphorescent sea creatures, enthused by the whirling propeller, marked the vessel's southbound course.

A moonless sky embraced a night destined for dark deeds and the voracious ocean would consume all sins.

According to a placemat he'd stolen from the *Fly Strip*, Dick calculated he was about six miles offshore and it looked like the water should be hundreds of feet deep.

He killed the *Dog's* diesel engine and tossed his backpack and cooler into the dinghy, climbed in, tied them securely then checked his pocket for the insurance policy.

Finding everything in order, Dick jumped back onboard and dropped into the dark, dank cabin to commit the final deed.

He went directly to the head and located an exposed hose under the toilet. Although easy to access, the ribbed rubber tube presented unexpected resistance.

"Damn hose is tougher than a hungry tick," Dick mumbled and jerked spasmodically. "Don't get a hernia fool, use your knees, eh!"

Without warning the hose snapped free and smacked Dick in the face.

"SACRE BLEU!"

Dick dropped the hose and turned to abandon the flooding cabin. He backed up and touched a soft object. It was a dark shape, a shape like a freaking foot!

Cold, and still slippery from Naldo's blood, the appendage poked out from under mildewed sail bags in the forward cabin. Dick jerked away and stared at his hand in the shadowy cabin, blood!

By now, the water was up to his ankles and Dick snapped out of it, yet for an instant, he swore he could smell baked goods. Weird. He thought about putting the hose back on and checking this out but the *Faulty Dog* had already commenced her death roll.

Afraid he might go down with the ship, Dick scooted topsides as the old sloop embraced her last sky. "Drowning is not my cup of tea, eh," Dick said to himself and climbed into the dinghy. He stared at his bloodied fingers, "A bloodstained foot? Oh, well, not my problem, eh."

Dick, not one to ponder the imponderable, cracked a beer instead. Pumped up on hops and adrenalin he didn't notice a small tug and tow a mile away in the darkness. Dick rinsed his bloody hand in the warm seawater. "I did it! I freakin' did it! Not bad for an amateur."

He leaned back, took a hearty guzzle and laughed at the faceless night. He thought he smelled bird shit but soon forgot the fast fading stench.

Scuttling a boat is like murder, he'd concluded, without a body it's hard to prove.

17

Just before the cabin went underwater the dinghy jerked forward, pulled by the bowline attached to the sinking *Dog*.

"Holy Mother of Moose, I forgot the bow line, it's still tied off, eh!" The surprised rubber dinghy stood on end and was pulled half way below the surface. The pressure relief valves farted like an old trail horse on a downhill run. Dick held onto the outboard motor and prayed.

Fortunately, Dick's granny knot failed and the dinghy bounced back to the surface. A shrill "Aieee!" echoed across the water as a sucking sound escaped from a hole in the sea. Only crystal bubbles and a circling dorsal fin remained witness to the passing.

After the dinghy stopped rocking, Dick cracked another beer. "Whew, a close one calls for a cold one, eh." He toasted the empty sky.

After drinking most of the brew in one gulp, he started the engine, grabbed the hand held radio and hailed the Coast Guard on channel 16.

"Hello, hello, Mayday, Mayday."

"Vessel calling Mayday, vessel calling Mayday, this is United States Coast Guard, Station Key West. What is your position and nature of distress? Over."

"My boat, the *Faulty Dog,* took on water and sank. I'm safe, but all my shit is gone," he reported.

"Have you abandoned ship? Over."

"No, I didn't abandon any of my shit. It all sank with the boat and if anybody finds it it's still my shit, by the law of the sea, right, eh?"

"Ah, captain, where are you and where is your vessel? Over."

"I'm here and the boat is gone."

"Do you have a position? Over."

"Yes, I'm sitting down."

"No, I mean a landmark. Over"

18

"Sacre Bleu!"

"Yes sir, there is a red light, which is in front of me, and it's somewhere around Skinny Mon Key, which is to my left, I think, eh."

"What? Over."

"Don't worry Coast Guards, I've got a dinghy and will head back to shore on my own bottom, eh."

When the Coast Guard called back, Dick tossed the radio overboard, cracked another beer and cranked the throttle full speed ahead. The fat grey dinghy raced toward the twinkling shore, like a beagle to a bowl.

QUAID

The next day, the phone rang in the office of *Butler's Slow Boat Towing and Salvage.*

Quaid Butler's mobile office consisted of a pickup truck, two pairs of deep-pocket cargo shorts, a knife, a condom, a cell phone, hand sanitizer and a copy of Carol Lazar's book, *Brilliant Thoughts*; it didn't take up much room. He'd been in Key West and in the salvage business since returning from Vietnam.

On this day, his office was perched on the porch of the *Gran Vin Wine Bar and Poodle Fondling Parlor.*

A sweaty T-shirt imprinted with the words, *"Confidence-The feeling you have before you understand what is really happening,"* clung to Quaid's back like a drunken divorcé.

Quaid rocked onto his left cheek and dug deep for his vibrating cell phone. The disco ring tone, "Oh yes, it's Ladies Night," echoed from his crotch. He'd always had trouble getting the cell out of his pocket in a gentlemanly fashion.

"Slow-Toat Bowing and Salvage, Quaid Butler on the wire," an embarrassed Quaid said after retrieving the phone.

"Quaid Butler, it's really, really good to hear your voice."

The call was from a local insurance agent, Peter "Cole" Slaw, "The price just went up, Cole."

"You funny, Quaid, you funny, listen, one of my clients, a fuckwad named Dick McCreedy, just called to report his newly insured, *newly like yesterday*, sailboat, the *Faulty Dog*, sank outside the reef between Big Mon and Skinny Mon Key last night. You know where that is, Quaid?"

"You betcha, Red Rider, pulled a lot of bones off that reef."

"Ah, anyway, McCreedy told me that he and the *Faulty Dog* set forth on her maiden voyage and quote, 'She was fully loaded, provisioned and equipped for a trip to the Bahamas and maybe,' Cole changed voices, 'the entire whole world. Then she sank,' unquote. McCreedy said it would be the trip of his lifetime. Dick's voice trembled when he talked, Quaid. Then he said, 'And now,' he says, 'Now, I've lost everything!' "

"Nice impersonation, Cole."

"Thanks man, I'm trying out for the Fringe Theater, I..."

"Cole, heel!"

"Anyway, McCreedy requested immediate and full payment of thirty-fuckin' K! Plus, get this Quaid, a *refund* of his premium! The nerve!" Quaid noted Cole's voice also trembled as he spoke.

"I'm going to give McCreedy your number, Quaid, and when he calls you tell him you are going to FIND his freakin' boat. Tell him it's a piece of cake. Tell him you do it every day. *Nolum probnolum,* that's Latin, that type of thing, OK? See what he says then let me know, will ya?"

"Roger on that and Cole, how about some money up front on this one, old pal?"

"I'll get back to you on that. It's a matter for the committee."

"Right."

"Quaid, let me ask you, do you feel confident about finding the boat?"

"Yeah, Cole," he glanced at his sweat sodden T-shirt, "at this point I feel confident."

"You don't sound too excited, Quaid."

"I'm not."

After three years of back to back in the bush with an Army Special Warfare team in Vietnam and a date with the last dance in *Vung Tau,* Quaid's nature embodied the view, "Once you've survived a war, everything else is anticlimactic."

For an instant, he remembered boarding a grey transport plane in Vietnam headed back to the States. Over the combined sighs of relief from almost two hundred survivors and the sound of jet engines spooling up, he heard the crew chief say, "Welcome aboard ladies, anybody still alive? Don't worry; you'll be home by this time yesterday."

There was no booze on the trip home so Quaid reflected on his stretch in the bush and realized he'd survived more by instinct than by intellect. He'd have to bear that in mind.

The next day Quaid received a phone call and after another embarrassing pocket pursuit answered, "Go ahead, this is Quaid Butler here, on the horn."

"Ah, hello? This is Dick McCreedy."

"Dick?"

"Hello to you, Mr. Quaid. I heard that you are going to go out and find my boat, eh. Can you do that?"

"Yep, we sure can, Dick. It's a cakewalk! Do it every day. *Nolum probnolum,* that's Latin for no problem, Dick. Can you tell me where it is?"

"Nope, not really, it's out there pretty far, in the water, you know."

"How far?"

"Pretty ... far."

"Well, don't worry young fella we'll find her and bring her up so you can fulfill your dream."

"Huh? You can do that? It's probably pretty deep ... in the water ... deep."

"Yes, we can and we will. Can and will, young fella, that's the ticket, Can and Will."

"Fuck."

"What's that? You're breaking up."

"I said, Good Luck!" Dick replied and hung up.

The wily McCreedy began a rapid and unplanned migration north, north to his chilly home in Mule Hump, Ontario and legendary birthplace of Nanook of the North.

The same day Quaid got the job, Cole also assigned a marine investigator named Zen "The Kut" Kutner to pursue the case.

According to the Coast Guard, the tug *Missus Wilkes* passed near Skinny Mon Key when the *Faulty Dog's* Mayday call went out. Because a Mayday call indicates immediate distress, the captain, Spud Pooley, took quick radar bearings on a tiny target near Skinny Mon Key that he thought might be the *Faulty Dog*. *Missus Wilkes* was a deep draft ocean going tug with a tow on a wire. She could not come closer or render assistance at the time. Captain Pooley reported this information to the Coast Guard that night, after Dick had thrown his radio overboard, then continued his voyage northward.

With the information provided by the US Coast Guard, whose only job is safety at sea and who have no interest in salvage, The Kut located the *Missus Wilkes* in Savannah, Georgia where she'd commenced unloading a barge filled with 200-tons of sunbaked, salt-sprayed, premium Bahamian guano.

"The *Missus Wilkes* proved easy to locate," The Kut wrote in his cryptic report, "everyone just held their noses and pointed upwind."

The Kut, a multi-talented rogue, talked to a few dockhands and stevedores and eventually tracked Captain Pooley to a bordello/snack bar near the unloading docks. He listened to Captain Pooley tell the same story he'd told the Coast Guard, but The Kut also got a set of radar bearings from that night. The interview ended abruptly when Pooley, a two-hundred-fifty-pound Down-Easter with a face that looked like an abandoned piece of macramé, responded to an unasked question. He spoke loudly through his nose.

"Lookee here, Mister Kut, this here's some good shit, Bahamian bird shit and Bahamian bird shit is for the rich organic type folks you know, and well, they like it fresh, Kut, so Pooley's gotta go."

~ ~ ~

After three days on a Greyhound bus, Dick McCreedy crossed the Canadian border. He didn't think the bad guys would follow him to, "Nanook of the North" country. Who goes to Canada except Canadians, he wondered and went to find the nearest border bar. He frowned as he sat down; I'll miss the warm weather, eh, and ordered a draft beer at Donny Gurner's, *Suck-It-Up-Pub*.

~ ~ ~

Dick made a few phone calls to Gorton's Marina during his pilgrimage north. Unfortunately, he learned the search for his boat continued in earnest. The more he thought about his actions, the more paranoid he became.

After a few pints of, *The Back of God's Hand Stout*, he bought some herb from the bartender and rolled a fatty with Manitoba Goose Weed. After a few nose to toes tokes, he obtained a pocketful of coins from a nearby Laundromat and called Quaid from a payphone.

"Ah, hello ... Mister Quaid?"

"Hey, Dick, is that you? Quaid Butler here."

"Ah, yes and, well, Quaid, I been drinking, ah, I mean, thinking on things and last night I talked with God and, and ... well, God said that you guys shouldn't have to pay for anything because it was ... an act, an act of God ... of God, Quaid ... really."

"God said that?"

"Yeah, pretty much. We, actually, He talked last night you know, and so, you know, I just called to say, ah … Goodbye." The phone clicked.

I live in a land of shipwrecks and dipsticks, Quaid thought. He hummed along with the dial tone for a few seconds, improvising a salty rift, then hung up and called Cole.

"Cole, McCreedy called and said he talked with God last night."

"He what?"

"He talked with God."

"Oh … Hey! Get his call back number off your phone and send it to me! We'll put The Kut on his bones!"

"Roger, Cole. Anyway, listen, God told Dick that you shouldn't have to pay for the boat because, according to Him, God, that is, the sinking was an act of God."

"You're shitting me, right?"

"Negative."

"What a flapping wing nut, and a lousy crook too. God! He talked to the Great Adjuster in the sky! My ass! It's an act all right and it's got nothing to do with God. Tell him to send me a note saying … let's see … 'I, Dick McCreedy, talked with God and God said, No Claim.' Tell him to get it notarized just in case."

"Got it, Cole."

"And Quaid, go find that freakin' boat, we're gonna give Dick a trip to jail as a policy bonus."

THE SEARCH.

The forty-foot salvage vessel, *Betty's Boongy,* with three SOB's (souls on board,) glided through a calm sea. Damp, stinky-pink, paper cascaded from a side-scan sonar machine mounted in the cabin and diesel exhaust fumes invaded the cramped space, like a fart in a deep-sea suit. It had been ninety degrees for three days with no breeze. Everything smelled bad.

On deck, the first mate, Tombolo, who said his name meant, "A dry hump between two wet spots," in Portuguese, stood watch while "Stinky Jim" Henndick, a retired Navy side scan sonar operator, hired for this particular job, adjusted a cluster of knobs and dials.

"Damn paper reeks, don't it?" Quaid remarked as he adjusted the throttle and autopilot.

"Yup, it sure do, don't it? Your mate Tombolo doesn't seem to be bothered by it though." Jim said.

"Yeah, I noticed, he's a tough guy." Quaid said.

Jim couldn't smell the paper anymore but felt compelled to show compassion for those who could. He didn't notice the wads of gum stuck in Tombolo's nostrils.

Tombolo Hicks had worked with Quaid on and off for ten years. He was the guy who received "the call," when things got nasty and was one of several waterfront clan members who saved Quaid's ass on a regular basis. It was one of the reasons, Quaid said, he would never leave the Keys.

The WW II, battery powered, side-scan sonar unit hummed quietly and received electronic signals from a

26

torpedo-like tube called a fish. The fish, towed on a reinforced wire behind *Betty's Boongy*, sent information to a stylus that, in turn, scratched the information onto a ten-inch wide roll of damp, stinky-pink paper. The fish had to be towed about twenty-feet off the bottom. The paper printout required constant observation by Jim and an equal effort by Quaid to keep the fish out of the mud.

By 6:00 PM on the third day, the crew had thirty-six hours invested in the search. Jim stared continuously at the pink paper to avoid missing the small image of a sailboat that could appear at any moment. All efforts were wasted if he glanced away and missed the target.

For three 12-hour days, Quaid sat in the helm chair. His butt surrendered itself to gravity and molded to the chair and his eyes, tired from staring at the NAV gear, fought to stay open. Hour after hour, speed and heading remained constant. The turns were particularly difficult. One mistake and the fish might augur into the silt, become entangled, or worse, lost. After three days of soreness, hungriness and soberness, Quaid was tired and ready to call it quits.

"This is tiresome," Quaid said.

"I know." Jim stared at the stinky paper. After three days there wasn't much else to say.

The setting sun tee'd up on the horizon like God's own golf ball and with His perfect putt rolled into the hole of another day somewhere around the world. It would be dark before they recovered the gear and returned to Key West.

"There it is!" Jim cried, "There THE FUCK it is!"

On the paper, a half-inch high shape of a sailboat appeared in white.

'What the 'uck!" Tombolo said.

Tombolo lost his four front teeth years ago when a moray eel snatched a regulator out of his mouth and tried to mate with it. He'd had trouble pronouncing F's ever since. Quaid turned towards Tombolo and grinned, "Drop the mark, Bolo! Drop!"

Tombolo, a part time employee, on call 24/7, who liked to introduce himself as an *On-Call-O-Gist*, threw a pre-rigged weight with float and line off *Betty's Boongy's* transom. The ten-pound lead ingot thankfully missed the tow wire and quickly found the bottom. After several passes they adjusted the mark and the stinky- pink confirmed that the *Faulty Dog* sat upright on the bottom in two-hundred-six-feet of northbound Gulf Stream water, one-half mile south of Skinny Mon Key.

After they recovered the fish and cable the crew jumped up and down, slipped on the slimy paper and hugged each other to prevent falling. There is nothing like success and they were a joyous trio. Tombolo pulled the chewing gum plugs out of his nose and cracked three beers; Stinky Jim rubbed his eyes and stretched and Quaid grinned like a fool while flexing his buttocks. Success! Everyone cheered and hammered down a cold one. It was a good day.

~ ~ ~

The next morning Quaid, Tombolo and another deep-air diver, Billy Beanne, met aboard *Betty's Boongy.*

Benjamin "Billy" Beanne, one of the first sport divers to test the limits of mixed gas deep dives had worked with the experimental diving community for years and survived. Born on the island of Key West, he noticed early on that most people who had money were the same ones who took all the risks. From then on, life was just simple math for Beanne.

Quaid laid out the bones of the job.

"OK, Beanne, we got to go down to two-oh-six and find a sinker, could be a scuttle."

"We gotta go down, but we don't gotta come up, that sort of a thing, right, Quaid?"

"Roger that, Beanne, the cardinal rule."

"OK, when?"

"Now."

"I figured as much. I guess we ought to plan the dive, and we ought to dive the plan," Beanne reminded Quaid with a friendly elbow to the ribs, "and we ought to calculate our decompression stops and we ought to make notes on our wrist boards and ..." Quaid sometimes thought Beanne suffered from oughtism.

During their preparations they remembered to include Martini's Law in the calculations. Martini's Law is a simple calculation. It suggests that, "Every thirty feet in water depth is the equivalent of drinking one martini," to explain the effects of nitrogen narcosis, the Rapture of the Deep.

Today would be a six-martini dive. Quaid and Beanne were the olives.

Onboard the *Boongy,* eight bottles of compressed air lined the gunwales. Going and coming from two-hundred-feet they would need most of it. The divers had only three minutes of bottom time to complete the search of the *Faulty Dog* and determine why she sank. Three minutes during which the divers would be under the wicked-fun influence of nitrogen narcosis, the Rapture of the Deep. Beanne liked deep air, Quaid liked it more.

They arrived at the coordinates and marker buoy was still in place, no one had stolen it, good luck so far.

Quaid and Beanne mentally prepared for the two-hundred-six-foot descent to the wreck. A working dive, on air, to two-hundred-feet is not for the weak or undetermined. For most divers, nitrogen narcosis sets in around ninety feet.

This is freakin' nuts, Quaid reminded himself in the same manner that he prepared for many of the things he did which were, in all fairness, freakin nuts.

He fitted his flippers, snorted his snorkel and fitted a wrist board to his right arm. Beanne did the same.

Tombolo guided them back to the exact position and dropped the anchor near the marker buoy. *Boongy's* color video fish finder showed they were directly over the *Faulty Dog*.

After checking each other's gear, Quaid and Beanne donned their masks and fell backwards into the patient sea. Hand over hand they pulled themselves down the anchor line, securing fresh dive tanks, each with its own regulator, at three different depths for the decompression stops on the way back up. Luckily, they snagged the anchor in the *Faulty Dog's* rigging, luck that saved valuable bottom time getting to the wreck.He knew the head compartment provided the easiest access to hoses or valves that could be used to scuttle the *Faulty Dog*. He would go there first.

It took only a few minutes to reach the sea floor.

"Burgll ... urgllrr ... burgll ..." Quaid said to Beanne as they passed through ninety feet.

"Burrglr, burgle urglee," Beanne replied. They grinned like idiots, nodded like idiots and wordlessly deemed this dive, "Freakin Nuts."

At two hundred feet, the water was colder than an ex-wife's handshake, visibility about one hundred feet. A light current pushed the tropical effluvia northward towards Newfoundland and the cold stoned beaches of Western Europe.

The *Faulty Dog* sat on a flat, sandy bottom. A heavy lead keel kept her upright during the descent and her loose main sail flapped slowly in the current, as if she were trying to sail away. Quaid looked at Beanne, pointed at his own head and made a stupid face.

Beanne laughed. He knew what it meant. It meant Quaid narced-out at ninety, but Beanne didn't care, he'd also narced at ninety.

Beanne flippered to the bottom and squatted over a sea cucumber that looked like a big green turd, he pretended to take a dump to get a laugh from Quaid.

"Hhorgl shorgl!" ... They were having fun now!

Fortunately, the men were trained divers and remembered to read the dive plan strapped to their wrists. Quaid nodded at Beanne and entered the small cabin. Beanne remained outside and rode the Rapture of the Deep.

Quaid's flippers stirred fine grey silt that swirled and fogged the already dark cabin. He worked his way forward. A large Nassau grouper exploded out of the darkness and thumped past Quaid's face. He could hear both his, and the grouper's bones crack, in mortal fear. Narced to the gills, Quaid spooked, sucked saltwater and gagged. Gagging is considered poor form at two-hundred feet.

Quaid forcibly regained control of his breathing and tried to find the space where the marine toilet was located. He peered into the darkness and felt his way along the inside contours. When he located the head, he opened the door, pushed the button on his underwater light and there, next to the toilet, lay a loose hose and two dangling hose clamps. The hose had been pulled off the sea valve and allowed immediate flooding. Quaid pulled a waterproof camera out of his buoyancy compensator and snapped flash pictures of the hose. He checked his wrist board and watch, thirty seconds to exit the cabin and begin his ascent. The flashlight flickered and then went off. "Furg!"

Quaid reached into the half-light to steady himself. He turned, felt something slippery, leaned in closer and saw foot, a human foot. "Hurgle, nurgle, hee!" Quaid burbled. It meant, "HELLO, maybe I'm a little NARCED HERE!" The slippery foot-like appendage felt slimy, but looked like a foot nonetheless. Quaid squeezed, it even felt like a foot! He chuckled and tickled the appendage. "Burbble, eurble (coochi-coo)!" Common sense ascended with his bubbles, it was Deep Air at its best.

Narced to the gills, Quaid somehow thought the person whose foot he held might still be alive. His Cub Scout training kicked in and he pulled the foot back toward open water. Billy Beanne would know what to do.

The silt, thicker now from the ruckus, made visibility much worse and to top it off the foot seemed attached to a weird looking body, a body that began to rise unexpectedly through the companionway hatch.

Quaid, six-feet tall, one hundred eighty pounds and no spring chicken, wrestled violently to gain control of the body, but it kept going up. His breath came in gasps and his mask fogged up. Fucker must be bloated and full of gas Quaid reckoned as his ass was dragged toward the surface. Some black, net-like, material tangled in the regulator behind his head. He couldn't get away! He found his dive knife, but dropped it, as he accelerated. Quaid focused. He knew he must force himself to exhale all the way to the surface, or explode and die. Poor form again.

Water rushed past and tried to pull his mask off. He ascended faster than his bubbles. Fuck! Black lace?

While Quaid held this discussion with himself, Billy Beanne watched his dive buddy rocket past with a slowly expanding body-like thing above his head. Away from the anchor line, Quaid couldn't stop himself and raced toward the surface, his bubbles expanding into thousands more on the way up.

"Urgllee Wo Urgllee-(Let Her Go, Let Her Go!")" Beanne mouthed and laughed like an idiot. He knew Quaid couldn't hear him and everything seemed funny. Beanne was narced to the gills as well.

"Blork y gork, Blork y gork! (Blow and Go! Blow and Go!")" Beanne mouthed then quickly focused and forgot about Quaid when he realized he'd have to ascend soon and slowly or get the bends and die a painful death himself. Thanks to the Rapture of the Deep, even that possibility seemed hilarious.

At twenty feet, the still expanding body broke free. In a desperate attempt to save the victim, Quaid grabbed wildly and detached two, somehow familiar, red objects.

On the surface, a moment of madness ensued. Quaid popped to the surface and tore his mask off. "I'm fucked!" he cried as a distended, partially inflated, love doll floated tits-up nearby. The doll bobbed towards Quaid, he saw the black mesh stockings that had entangled his regulator. "Damn it!"

Tombolo grabbed a boat hook and poked at the doll. Quaid heard a pop as Jim dragged him out of the water and laid him on his back like a frog in biology class.

"Rum?" Tombolo inquired and avoided looking at the red latex objects in Quaid's hands while *Conchita* sank slowly out of sight; her unblinking, painted plastic eyes stared serenely at the tropic sky.

After two short decompression stops, Beanne appeared on the surface and gave the OK sign. Everyone on *Betty's Boongy* began laughing. Beanne grinned; the laughter told him Quaid must have made it. Then he realized why the all the yuks, the love doll was draped over *his* head now and looked like an octopus with red Botoxed lips. The scene was as funny as a fart in a sauna, until Quaid started moaning.

"OK, I guess the party's over." Tombolo sighed. Quaid's getting soft, he thought, picked up the VHF radio microphone and hailed the Coast Guard on Channel 16. Beanne flopped down on the deck beside Quaid.

"Some ride, huh?"

"You betcha, Beanne."

"U.S. Coast Guard, U.S. Coast Guard this is Tombolo onboard *Betty's Boongy*. Come in. We gotta a deep air prune here! Need an ambulance, a chamber, and bring some Cokes! We're headed to the Toxic Triangle, Pronto! Out!"

Tombolo cut the anchor line to save time. It sank to the bottom with five full dive tanks still attached. Beanne had used only one to make his ascent.

Jim gave Quaid a bottle of emergency oxygen to suck on while Tombolo punched the throttle full ahead and put his ear protectors on so he wouldn't be forced to listen to Quaid's lament. *Betty's Boongy* blew black smoke and raced for shore.

THE PRESS

Back at the dock, Quaid Butler sat on a rotted wooden dock box. With Billy Beanne's help, he'd changed into his cargo shorts and shirt on the way in so he could off-gas through his skin. He couldn't stop twitching and itching. He heard crackling heat from the hot diesel engine, he knew Tombolo had run her full speed all the way in trying to save his ass. Quaid scratched himself as nitrogen gas escaped through his skin, it itched like mix of sunburn and poison ivy. He waited anxiously for an ambulance to arrive.

Forty-five minutes ago he'd been two hundred feet under water at 6.08 atmospheres. Now, at 1.0 atmosphere, sea level, his body was under assault. He looked at his trembling hands and involuntarily off-gassed, "Damn nitrogen," he explained to a nearby gecko. He reached into his pocket and withdrew the red rubber aureoles, his only reward so far. He remembered pulling them loose as he fought to control the doll. They were obviously meant to be detachable and looked like tiny party hats, a combination of top hat and sombrero. Although he no longer felt "confident," and would soon be crippled with pain, Quaid stared at the little red sisters. "Let's party!" he said with false bravado and a friendly tweak. Focus on the basics, Quaid reminded himself, then tweaked again.

An ambulance siren screamed like a pissed-off gull and grew louder. Quaid's crew looked on with concern. Everyone seemed OK, except for Quaid whose unplanned and rapid ascent from the *Faulty Dog* left un-purged and expanding nitrogen gas in his tissues and joints. They all knew the ride to the recompression chamber on Phleming Key would be a short and painful trip.

The ambulance arrived in a cloud of crushed oyster shells and coral dust. Two uniformed attendants jumped out and scooped Quaid into the vehicle. They strapped him to a stretcher, slapped an oxygen mask on his face and tried to pry the elastic nipples from his fingers. The little red cones stretched and then snapped back. Fighters! When the alpha medic stopped tugging, Quaid gave him one as a sign of friendship.

The medic nodded his thanks as the ambulance surged ahead. Beanne waved goodbye with a wet flipper. Back in *Boongy's* cabin, Tombolo rolled a bone with damp pink paper and passed it around, then aggressively, but mistakenly, took a hard hit on the empty O2 bottle and passed out, face first, in the crushed oyster parking lot.

~ ~ ~

"Press me quick man, it's starting to hurt bad!" Quaid said. The *Press* is what deep air divers call the recompression/decompression process.

The driver's quick acceleration threw the medic on top of Quaid. "Not that kind of press you fuck-wad! Gimme my nipple back," Quaid snapped. The medic's red face matched the nipple.

"You're still narced, sir." the medic said politely and stared at the colorful object remaining in Quaid's hand. "Want me to take that one too, sir?"

Quaid calmed, "Nope, it's all I got to show for my efforts so far, son."

"Oh." The medic climbed off Quaid and straightened himself, "That's a tough business you're in, sir."

"No shit."

The medic shrugged, he'd seen weirder.

The Key Lime green ambulance screeched to a stop at the U.S. Army Special Forces Underwater Operations

School where khaki clad attendants hustled Quaid into a double-lock recompression chamber. A different medic joined him in the chamber to oversee the recompression/decompression, the "Press," veteran divers called it.

"At least I remembered to blow and go instead of holding my breath on the way up. I would have exploded, ya know." Quaid told the medic.

"I know." The medic said.

"Still, the bends can last longer and are supposed to be more painful than exploding, ya know."

"I know."

"I'm lucky to be alive ..."

'I know."

Disappointed with the conversation, but comforted to have avoided being blown up, Quaid knew the pain would only increase as the Martini effect wore off. Still narced, Quaid chuckled to himself, "Guess I'll be going back through Narcsville on the way down. Giddy-up, or is it Giddy-down!"

It wasn't his first dance with deep air, but he knew it could be the last.

Outside the tempered glass port light, the chamber operator twisted valves and eyeballed needle gauges as the chamber pressurized to the equivalent depth of two-hundred feet. Hot metallic air hissed through pressure pipes like air brakes on a garbage truck.

Quaid hunched against the increasing heat. His bare thighs suction-locked on the stainless steel bench and he had trouble clearing his ears as they raced down six atmospheres. The medic watched him closely. Quaid held his nose, blew hard and hoped he could keep up with the rapid descent. He would breathe pure oxygen, on and off, for at least two hours during the press. He hoisted the tattered nipple in front of the glass viewing port like a religious talisman and gave the operator a thumbs-up. The chamber operator nodded, mouthed the words, "Blow and Go" and cranked the valves wide open.

With time to kill, "What just happened?' became question number one.

Question number two, less relevant but equally troubling, came to Quaid's mind as he passed through ninety feet. "Are Key West Roosters on Crack?" He remembered reading this headline in the local newspaper, the Mullet Wrapper. The article went on to say that local bartender and birdologist, Cory Carlson, noticed that whenever a cop car slowed in front of some gangstas hanging out on the street, the gangsta's threw a bunch of little white packets out of their pockets and ran. Before the cops could zip their flies, put down their *con leches* and get out of their cars, the roosters pecked up the packets and flew off.

According to Carlson, "That's why them roosters crow at all hours of the night, they don't know what time it is. They're wired man, stoned to the bone. It's Party Time! Know what I mean? The roosters' crow like that cuz they're higher than a frigate bird, know what I mean?"

Chickens on crack, the thought had never occurred to Quaid, and he wondered why. These were only two of many questions he would seek to answer over the next few hours on the press.

Quaid leaned back; the steel was soft, one hundred fifty feet and going down. "Welcome home," deep air hissed softly. The medic inserted his ear buds and nodded out.

Quaid leaned forward and hummed a few bars of Dylan's *"I'll Be Your Baby Tonight."* He sighed, put his head in his hands and ran throbbing fingers through his damp red hair. What next, he wondered?

Tink.

What was that? Quaid looked around. The ear-budded medic didn't seem to hear anything. Nothing in the chamber could go, *tink*. "Could just be narced," Quaid laughed.

Quaid relaxed, put his head back in his hands and stared at the spaces between his gnarled toes. There, straight down in the bottom of the puke trough, between the big toe and index toe on his right foot, he spied a sparkle It was the color of Dimple Sue's misty, green eyes. The object glinted fiercely green in the puke trough below the grated chamber floor. Quaid dropped the nipple, reached through the grate and retrieved the twinkling object with throbbing digits. A large multi-faceted, radiant green stone winked back at him. Emerald, Quaid knew emeralds; his ex-wife taught him about them. A spectrum of colors flashed around the chamber. Quaid held the stone toward the port light and just as suddenly withdrew it.

"Where did this come from?" he asked quietly and stuck the glinting stone in his ear for safekeeping. Somebody's sure as hell going to come looking for this little darling. Great.

TINK

A few blocks away Beanne sucked down his sixth beer and molested a tray of Apalachicola oysters at the Spooner Wharf Bar. Beanne was tired and worried about his friend, he knew from experience that the bends are bad.

The wind turned cool and Beanne inhaled the smongus breeze. It smelled like beer and began to blow harder onshore. Beanne put his elbows on the bar, leaned over and scratched his thumping head. Rain ought to cool things down, he thought, and I ought to get under a roof.

Tink. Beanne looked down and noticed a green sparkle amongst the defeated bivalves. He rummaged through the fallen mollusks and retrieved a green stone the size of a baby's molar. With his head over the oyster tray, Beanne ruffled his hair to see if there were any more *tinks.* A concerned waitress noticed Beanne's behavior and paused to check on him.

"You OK, Beanne?" she asked.

"Huh, oh yeah, hi, Dimple Sue, I'm okeydokey, just doing my hair, ha, ha, thanks for checking though." After she'd gone, Beanne inserted the stone into his right ear for safekeeping. It was an old diver's trick.

Bonterra

Offshore, a line of hard white clouds snapped like god's own dentures at the horizon. The advancing wind pressed up Dung Beetle Lane and parted white rayon curtains in the second floor suite of the Gripps Hotel. The Gripps is located in the gay arena, next door to a pigeon barn on Old Gooser's Lane, in downtown Key West. The

Gripps Hotel, a well-known secret hideout, perfectly suited the needs of one Senor Ignacio "Iggy" Bonterra, a leading member of the disreputable but indispensable *Taco Blanco* cartel. Drugs, dollars, dry cleaning and death were Bonterra's beezness.

The sea's fecund breath filled the suite unchallenged and rustled Senor Bonterra's loose fitting kimono. Seduced by the wet wind his oversized silk kimono swirled like a bullfighter's cape. The doorbell rang. Bonterra turned his voluminous *boongy,* Cuban for a woman's butt, to the wind.

Not drawn to the horizon or its masticating clouds, Bonterra instead peeked through a peephole that looked too much like the barrel of a gun for his comfort. Satisfied, he opened the door. "Naldy, Naldy, what good news do you bring?"

Naldo had taken a cab from the marina and looked rough. *"Muy malo, Senor, muy malo,"* Naldo squeaked and sniffed the pungent air.

Bonterra's bald head harbored eyes that focused on a rumpled man standing before him wearing a bloodstained tablecloth as a diaper and smelling of baked goods.

Bonterra shook his head, walked back into the room and hopped into a swivel chair. With a big ass and legs too short to reach the floor, he spun helplessly for a few seconds until his kimono caught in the wheels and he slowed to a stop. Through the glass-top desk, Bonterra saw blood on Naldo's legs. He also found Naldo to be less than perpendicular to the visible horizon, a visual anomaly that put him in an ominous mood.

For his part, Naldo tried to stand at attention, like a wounded tough guy in the movies, but with four bullets in his butt and one in his foot he could neither stand nor sit comfortably. He teetered in front of Senor Bonterra on bloody flip-flops that squished when he shifted his weight.

"So ... Naldy," Bonterra lit the wrong end of a fake Cuban cigar and coughed violently. His fat lips stuck together at the corners when he spoke.

"So, eet looks like you got shot in the ass. Am I close, Naldy?" Bonterra hacked up a ball of phlegm and spit it on the hard wood floor.

Naldo hated it when Bonterra called him Naldy. "Sí, Senor Bonterra."

"Anything you'd like to share about the unsightly perforations, like why? Eh?"

"Ah, I went for my fun, ah, gun and some guy shot me in the ass."

"Do you know *who* shot you in the ass? Do you know *why* someone shot you in the ass?"

"No, not really, really."

"How about really, really?"

"I do not know, Senor, maybe some guy got mad cuz I porked his muff. I never see who shoot me. Nobody knows I am in dee boat. I no have clue unless, unless eez that punk Raul."

"Oh shit! Not Raul Mims? *Madre del Idiota* ! You porked his muff?"

"Yeah, you know, I mean not really porked, just laid some pipe."

"Pipe? *Madre Dios!* Do you think only of making dee boom-boom? Look, Naldy, I want to know just one thing. Where are the fucking stones? Period. You can deal with Raul's dad, Bad Mingo Mims, on your own time. He's gonna come and get you, you know. Would you like a cigar?" Bonterra reached slowly into his desk drawer. Naldo noticed the sinister move.

"Ah, I, ah ..." The entire screwed-up day flooded in on Naldo like a leaking toilet in the apartment above. *Conchita's* hissing had been the hardest to bear. He'd tried to plug her bullet hole with cookie dough but only made it worse. Watching the slow deflation of a loved one is the same everywhere.

Naldo closed his eyes and waited for the bullet he knew would come. "I am ready to make the dying," he said with trembling voice. He crossed his fingers and closed his eyes but, being dyslectic, did the opposite and stood heroically poised to meet his maker, although he had no clue who his "maker " might be.

"And fuck you too, BONNIE!" Naldo belted out.

These were Naldo's parting words to his boss. He'd had enough of being called Naldy and would crumple to the dusty tongue and groove floor and bleed out with pride. He would die like a, a, a dying man.

After a few moments, Bonterra coughed politely to hide the silence. "Hey, Naldy, snap out of it. You're not dead yet, *comprendo?*" Bonterra compressed an evil fat lipped grin.

"Oh, sí ..." Naldo's eyes uncrossed and he immediately spilled his guts to hide his embarrassment. "They're in her special projects pocket. That's where they are. I swear!"

"Special projects pocket? What special pocket?"

"*Conchita's* pocket. She's my, ahh ... ahh ... assistant."

"Special projects pocket? You have an assistant?"

"Yes, she eez inflatable ..."

"You better fill me in, Naldy."

He did and after five minutes the situation became clear.

"So Naldy, you are saying the stones are in the rubber pussy of a wounded love doll named *Conchita*, in the cabin of a sailboat called the *Faulty Dog* at a place called Gorton's Marina? That means you don't have the stones, Naldy. Is that *correcto?*"

"Sí, Senor Bonterra you are right. Most very right! But, please to excuse me, I am bleeding ... Please, senor, a doctor."

"Thank you for your service, Naldy. I will help with your suffering."

"*Gracias ...*"

Bonterra pulled a silenced .357 magnum from his desk drawer and aimed it at Naldo. Naldo looked down the gun barrel, like a chicken down a line scratched in the dirt. He never heard the bullet, the bullet that missed his head, flew out the open window and embedded in a forgiving coconut tree. The scent of gun powder, cigar smoke and the peculiar odor of sudden fear embraced like old friends.

Naldo headed for the bathroom. Even a closed door and continual flushing could not deaden Bonterra's cruel guffaws.

When Bonterra stopped laughing, he picked up the phone and called in a favor. Within minutes his dentist, Billy Joe Hayfield, DDS, arrived shot Naldo up with Novocain, extracted the bullets and patched his riddled ass and foot. "Good thing you got a fat little Boongy, Naldy," Hayfield said, "Otherwise, you'd be totally, if not completely, dead by now."

Not convinced the remark constituted a compliment, Naldo remained silent.

Bonterra watched Naldo; he knew the Novocain would soon wear off. He whistled loudly through an embarrassing gap between his front teeth when he saw the bullet holes in Naldo's ass. "*Quattro,*" he noted.

The space between Bonterra's front teeth intrigued the dentist. Correcting it would be a lucrative job. He offered to fill the gap, but Bonterra seemed uninterested.

Bonterra whistled a second time and a three-hundred-pound Samoan entered from an adjacent room. Bonterra snapped his fingers to get Naldo's attention. "Naldy, this is Maytag."

The Samoan giant turned to a life of crime after failing to attain his dream of becoming an Olympic ski jumper. His attempt at pole vaulting was even more distressing.

"Maytag will help with the heavy lifting." Bonterra flipped Naldo a set of keys, "Take my car and Maytag and get those fucking stones. *Comprendo?*"

"What kind of car is it?" Naldo asked.

"Yugo."

"Ok, I'm going, I'm going, I just need to know what kind of car it is."

"*Madre Dios*! Maytag, get his riddled ass out of here."

"Hold on there, Senor Bonterra," Hayfield said. "This fool has lost a lot of blood and will draw too much attention if you send him out right now. He's a liability in his present condition. You have to keep him here for a few days before he will be of use to you. Lots of water, fresh fruits, fiber and ..."

"Get the hell out of here," Bonterra ordered and palmed the dentist five hundred bucks.

"Need a receipt?" Hayfield asked and stared longingly at Bonterra's gap.

Bonterra shook his head in disbelief.

He ignored the dentist's advice and decided that two hours of healing time would be sufficient for Naldo. Iggy reached for another fake Cuban. He wished he could send Maytag by himself, but the big guy wasn't the sharpest marble in the bag.

Two hours passed and lo, on the third hour, Naldo rose from the bed. Although tired and in pain, he knew the discomfort would be nothing compared to what Bonterra would do to him if he failed. After a quick shit, shower and shave, greatly complicated by his dyslexia, Naldo and Maytag headed for the marina.

"You two be back in two hours, Naldy," Bonterra said.

Naldo located the Yugo and made the short drive to Gorton's Marina. Maytag rode in the back seat. He filled the entire space.

"You're a big one," Naldo remarked as he rolled up on one cheek and checked his butt bandage for bloodstains.

"Ugga" Maytag replied.

When they arrived at Gorton's, Naldo had to squirt sunscreen on Maytag to get him out of the car. They walked down the dock. Naldo did not feel well.

"Oh no!" Naldo stopped suddenly, his already considerable pain increased. "Dee boat she is gone. Dee *Dog* no here. *Madre Dios!*" Naldo looked around and noticed an old salt sitting nearby.

The man, known as Fire Ant, had finally reached his quota of dead or wounded mosquitoes for the day and was about to leave when Naldo and Maytag approached.

"Excuse me Senor *Capitan*. Do you know where dee *Faulty Dog* is?"

Fire Ant leaned forward and squashed a palmetto bug with his bare foot. "Yup."

"You want to tell us where?"

"Nope."

"You want Maytag here to squeeze your head like a pimple until you do?"

"Nope."

Maytag leaned forward, shading Fire Ant with his corpulent shadow.

"So, you think you're a tough guy," said Naldo.

"Yup."

"*Tofa*," was all Maytag enunciated before a 50,000 volt Taser took him down. He landed like a manatee dropped from a rescue net. Naldo looked away and peeled off a twenty-dollar bill. He creased it down the middle, kept his distance turned and handed it to Fire Ant. Maytag convulsed quietly nearby.

"Please excuse dee rudeness of heem," Naldo nodded toward the groaning Samoan.

Fire Ant snatched the bill like a bonefish would a fly. "Look, matey, all I know is a guy named McCreedy bought that boat. She was here two hours ago, but she ain't here now. *Comprendo?* Maybe he went out to watch sunset, hope he knows how to sail her back in!"

"*Muchas Gracias.*" Naldo handed Fire Ant his card. "Call me if you hear anything," he said and rubbed his thumb and forefinger together in the Latin manner.

Naldo coaxed Maytag into an upright position. Maytag grabbed Naldo's head like the knob on a gentleman's walking stick and headed towards the car. Naldo didn't care for Maytag's familiarity but had no choice and then he passed out.

Maytag palmed Naldo's by the head with one hand and opened the Yugo's trunk. He flopped Naldo's bloody carcass on top of the spare tire and slammed the lid. When Maytag went to get in the car he was too big to fit into the driver's seat and had to call a tow truck to get himself and Naldo back to the Gripps Hotel.

SPOONER WHARF

By nine o'clock, Quaid was out of the chamber and released back into the wild. The same medic who rode in the ambulance earlier had confirmed Quaid's bodily functions, got him to sign a mental health release form and returned the gifted nipple. "It's part of a set, man. I can't accept it," he nodded solemnly. Quaid put one nip on each side of his library card and folded his wallet. He called Cole and told him what happened but said nothing about the stones.

Quaid walked past the military gate guard and headed towards the Spooner Wharf Bar. After more than three hours in the recompression chamber it was time for a beer.

Dusk arrived like a bait net thrown over the sky. Quaid paused beneath the only working street light on Caroline Street to adjust a flip-flop. Suddenly, the pavement darkened as a large figure passed between the light and Quaid. The man, as big as a stacked washer/dryer, moved silently past with a small man in his wake. Quaid secured his flip-flop and kept moving.

FIRE ANT

While absorbing a beer at the Fly Strip Bar, the coconut telegraph kicked into action and Fire Ant learned of Quaid Butler's success. He overheard a guy named Jim say he worked as a side-scan sonar operator and that he and Quaid had located the *Faulty Dog* in two-hundred-feet of water south of Skinny Mon Key.

Although he hated to get involved with other peoples' affairs, Fire Ant still loved the old *Dog* and wanted to find out what happened to her plus, he could use a few bucks. The Ant did not own a cell phone, went to a phone booth instead and pulled Naldo's card out of his shorts. He held the phone between his ear and shoulder and dug enthusiastically for change in his pockets.

Plink, plink and, after several rings, "Ha-loo, Naldo is here."

"Naldo, its Fire Ant."

"Si?"

"From what I hear, the *Faulty Dog* was took out and sunk by that dickhead McCreedy and I heard old Quaid Butler went out and found her in two hundred feet of water."

"Where is deez, Butter, now?"

"He keeps his boat over to the Key West Bight Marina. She's called *Betty's Boongy*."

"Where are you now, *Hoguera Fuego*?" Naldo asked.

"What's that mean?"

"Is meaning, Ant of Fire. "?

"Oh, cool. Anyway, I'm buzzing around the *Fly Strip*."

49

"*Bueno*, I will bring *dinero* soon, to you."

"Mucho grassy-ass," Fire Ant replied.

~ ~ ~

There was no way to contact Quaid on the military base, so Billy Beanne stayed at the Spooner, drinking, thinking and swatting flies, waiting to hear from him. Beanne stared at beer foam patterns in his glass. "This beer's got some legs to it," he mumbled and thought about his recent find. He didn't notice Quaid ease up behind him.

"Blow and Go ... Wild Man!"

Beanne went airborne and landed on a nearby poodle. "ARK! ARK! ARK!"

He turned, saw Quaid, laughed like a mad man and spilled his beer on the wiry dog.

"Freakin' Quaid man, Blow and Go, man! Blow and Go! You made it!"

"Yeah, it wasn't easy, had to get narced again on the press."

"Ooo-rah! Go Army! Too bad, man! Too bad! Hee hee."

They high-fived and slapped each other on the back.

"So, what'd I miss?" Quaid asked.

"Oh, nothing man, just sitting here eating oysters and waiting to see how you were doing and, just so you know, when I left the *Boongy*, Ol' Tombolo was sleeping with an ice bag on his face."

"Did he suck on that empty O2 bottle and go dirt diving again?

"Yup, never fails."

"He's gotta stop trying to get high like that ... I told him to check and see if there's any gas in the bottle before he takes a hit on it."

"I know you did, Quaid."

"Oh well, Tombolo has his ways and there's no point in confusing him."

"Something else Quaid. ... I scratched my head a little while ago," Beanne looked around with suspicious eyes, "and I heard a Tink sound. I looked down and found a green stone in my oyster tray."

"A *Tink* in your oyster tray?"

"Yeah, a *Tink*."

"A pearl?"

"Have you ever seen a green pearl? Pay attention Double O, it's a freakin' emerald."

"Hoo-boy Beanne, we in deep doo-doo now!"

"Huh?"

With a trust borne among deep air divers and other self-accredited fools, Beanne nodded and glanced around. He leaned close, pointed to his ear and showed Quaid his hidden green stone. Quaid nodded, glanced around and pointed to his own twinkling ear hole. Four eyes locked, which was hard to do, while staring at each other's ears. There were a few odd looks from the raw bar.

Like many divers, old friends, husbands and wives, Quaid and Beanne could communicate best by not speaking. Quaid nodded at Beanne and got a kink in his neck. Beanne nodded back and got dizzy. Both recognized they were too tired to think straight or even nod well and silently agreed to wait until tomorrow to figure this thing out. Without a word, a wink or any additional nods Beanne and Quaid left the Spooner and headed in different directions.

It was a time to pause, a time to stop nodding.

Ten minutes later, Quaid returned to the Spooner to get a beer and resume thinking. He couldn't think outside the bar tonight. He found Beanne sitting alone under a collection of stinky lobster balls. He'd also returned to resume thinking and had two beers in front of him. Beanne nodded. Quaid nodded, grabbed one and sat down.

"Damn balls stink." Beanne nodded backwards.

"Yup, and stop with the nodding, you're giving me a kink in my neck."

"You got it, Red Rider," Beanne nodded.

"Do you think anyone knows we got these stones?"

"If they don't, they will."

While Naldo and Maytag dropped some cash off to Fire Ant and then ambled down to the waterfront in search of *Betty's Boongy,* Beanne and Quaid chugged their last beer, looked at each other and nodded. "Stop it!" they said at the same time and grinned.

They paid the bill and headed toward *Betty's Boongy,* docked in the Toxic Triangle on the east side of Key West Bight. It was time to check on Tombolo and continue thinking, and drinking.

BETTY'S BOONGY

etty's Boongy wallowed slowly in fish-foamed water. Quaid and Beanne boarded the vessel and went into the cabin. Tombolo lay face down in a pool of water. Gear and equipment scattered everywhere.

"Look at ol' Bolo," Beanne nodded, "He musta' fallen out of the bunk. All the ice is melted ... Oh no! The beer might be warm!" Beanne poked a finger through Tombolo's thick, stringy, gray-blond hair and searched for a pulse. He felt a hole.

"He's been shot, Quaid. He's dead!"

At the same time, Quaid grabbed Tombolo's left ear and lifted his face off the deck.

"Ah, hah!" Quaid said. He plucked a tightly rolled piece of paper out of Tombolo's flattened nose and let go. Bolo's face made a wet kissing sound as it bounced on the deck. Tombolo snapped upright. "The 'uck I'm dead and get your nasty 'inger out of my ear, Beanne that hurts. Gimme a cigarette, will ya?"

"Sorry Bolo, but you weren't breathing, I didn't feel a pulse," Beanne fired back.

"There's no pulse in your ear hole, for 'uck's sake." Tombolo snapped.

Quaid unrolled the wrinkled, foul smelling pink note written on left over sonar paper, "We knowing you got dee stones, Butter," Quaid read, "Give em' the fuck-back or dye."

"You boys been a-drinking, right, am I right?" Bolo asked.

"Nope." Beanne barked.

"Yup." Quaid said. "Who are these people, Bolo?"

Tombolo lit another lung harpoon and coughed, "Look, Quaid, the ice bag broke and I got up to take a whiz. Something got stuck in my 'lip-'lop. I heard it scraping on the deck and when I 'lipped my 'lop I spied a green stone stuck in the rubber. It scratched the deck, Quaid, must be real hard. I scooped it up and dropped it in an empty beer bottle so's I wouldn't lose it. It made a *Tink* sound when it hit the bottom."

Quaid and Beanne exchanged glances.

"Luckily, I hid the bottle in the garbage just be'ore two mean-looking guys came onboard."

Tombolo paused for breath.

"What happened?" Beanne asked needlessly.

"Well, the little 'ella says, 'Where eez dee stone?' I was smart enough to act dumb."

Quaid and Beanne rolled their eyes as Tombolo held up two nicotine stained fingers on each hand to indicate a quote.

"I said, check this out, I said, 'What 'ucking stones?' Genius, right! That's when the big 'ella grabbed my hair and dragged me into the cabin. I tried to kick him in the balls but got him in the belly instead, almost lost my 'oot. Anyway, then he pushed my 'ace onto the deck. That bummed me out. I don't think the dude meant to knock me out, but he did. It looks like they trashed the *Boongy* pretty bad. I don't know how long I've been lying here."

Quaid and Beanne fingered their ears and locked eyes for an instant. Tombolo caught the look.

"You know, i' it sparkles and makes a *Tink* when you drop it in an empty beer bottle, it must be good, right?"

Tombolo scuttled to the galley and after digging through a surprising number of empties, pulled a Key Deer Beer bottle from the refuse and shook it. "Put the little 'ucker in here for security keeping," he smiled. There were a series of *Tinks,* muted by glass, but *Tinks* nonetheless.

"Fuck."

"Shit."

"What ...? You boys know where it came 'rom, don't cha, don't cha?" Tombolo cocked his head with a snaggle-toothed grin, "It's a *Coup d'chance."* Silence abounded.

"I got a stone too." Beanne finally admitted.

"Me too," Quaid said.

"Must be the doll, right? Right, am I right? I knew I shouldn't have poked her. Still, she'll be the first one I regret letting go ..." Tombolo laughed and reached into the cooler. *Phssst ... Phssst ... Phssst.* They talked and drank until sleep sailed in.

BABY RAD'S

Morning came quicker than a boy scout in a whorehouse. A beer can rolled across the deck, its dizzying revolutions slowed only by splotches of early morning bird shit. Quaid, Beanne and Bolo shook themselves awake and wondered if it was yesterday yet.

Quaid and Beanne stuck a finger in their respective ears and nodded. Tombolo shook his beer bottle. Tink, Tink. It was real all right. No words were spoken as they ambled up Ballyhoo Lane for breakfast at *Baby Rad's* diner.

The trio looked like a drunken tripod and scuffled in still feeling the effects of too much cheap beer. Together they inhaled the scent of bacon and eggs with a hint of Tidy Bowl and stared at the percolating Bunn coffee machines, like lifeboats on the horizon. Quaid grabbed a booth near the bathroom, just in case.

"What we gonna do, Quaid?" Tombolo looked at Beanne.

"Ah, Bolo," Beanne nodded to his right and pointed, "that's Quaid, over there."

"Oh sorry, 'orgot my glasses, blind in one eye and can't see out of the other, ha, ha, anyway, what's the plan?" Tombolo skinny elbows slid apart on the greasy red Formica table. He caught himself in the nick of time. His bony frame and stringy muscles quivered in anticipation of caffeine. "I like caffeine, nico-tine and adrena-leen," he liked to say.

No one had any ideas, let alone plans. They stared at the upside down ketchup bottle with drunken devotion, and tried to read the label, each grateful that no one nodded.

Moonbeam, the waitress, riding a two-hundred-eighty-pound ass out of Winnipeg, Canada, approached the booth. She cocked back on one leg, pulled out her pad and rested it on her belly.

"You boys gonna eye-fuck all morning or get some grub in ya?"

Moonbeam had seen enough hangovers to last a lifetime. Committed drunks brought them in like stinky dogs and expected her to pet them. "No sir'ee, Bob," she told them, "not here, not now, not me."

There would be neither buffoonery nor sympathy while Moonbeam remained on duty.

"Oops, sorry Moonbeam, we was just thinking about our emer ... ah ... emmm, my aunt Emily, right, Quaid? Beanne said.

"Right, Beanne." Quaid exhaled and ordered breakfast for the three of them.

Beanne lapped his *café con leche*, like a cat drinking water, "What have you got us into, Quaid? This could be messy. You think there ought to be more stones on the bottom? Do they belong to that McCreedy guy? Those goons looked like they mean business. Whoever flattened Bolo thinks we got em' and they'll be back. Right so far, Quaid?"

"Ah ..."

"Quaid!"

"I've been thinking on it and it seems we got two choices," Quaid said. "We can take the *Boongy*, head out to the Tortugas, eat sand, lay low and die of boredom, or each other's company, or we can gear up and go look for the rest of the stones. No one else can find them 'cept us.

All for One and Screw'em All!" Quaid raised an imaginary beer, a cheerful toast from the head fool.

"Huh? Anyway, how do you know there's more?" Beanne burped.

"I don't, but you want to sit there on your dead ass and say there isn't?"

"I'm down with the screw'em part," said Tombolo.

"OK, me too," Beanne chimed, "Screw'em all!"

For some men, the thought of treasure, of unearned riches is more powerful than common sense. That's what makes it fun.

Quaid, Beanne and Bolo laughed loudly and high fived over the table. Without warning a large hand clamped over their upheld hands and squeezed. A large arm, attached to the large hand, jerked them onto their feet.

"What the fuck?" was rendered in painful harmony by the dangling participants. Suspended over the table, Quaid, Beanne and Bolo could only stare at each other's arm pits and curse.

Naldo appeared behind Maytag and eyeballed Tombolo. "So, now you no feeling so beeg, Meester Ice Bag? Eh? *Sì?* No?" Naldo nodded and Maytag dropped the three into their seats then squeezed in next to Tombolo. Naldo remained standing. Moonbeam delivered breakfast.

"Hey you, *Gordo*, get your fucking belly off my table." Moonbeam gestured at Maytag with a calloused elbow.

Maytag couldn't see the part of his anatomy she was pointing at and remained seated to avoid confusion. He tried to be helpful, but mistakenly pointed towards his crotch with a questioning look.

"Ugga?" He winked at Moonbeam.

Quaid, Beanne and Bolo looked down, said nothing and took quick, big bites. They knew what Moonbeam was capable of and chewed with silent resolve as the second hand on the wall clock stopped moving.

Moonbeam took a deep breath, put the breakfast plates down and exhaled. Frightened pancakes fluttered and moved away.

Well, that gesture, that hideous wink, combined with too many previous incidents set Moonbeam off and before you could say *over-easy*, she lit into Maytag with a handful of condiments and hot coffee. Quaid and Beanne bailed. Maytag struggled to stand and the small booth came apart. Tombolo vaulted straight up like a clutched grapefruit seed. Moonbeam grabbed two squeeze bottles of something and fired them up Maytag's nostrils, then slapped him ferociously with a breakfast menu. Maytag turned purple and went into a spin cycle.

Naldo stepped back. The ambush seemed to be going badly, no sense in a futile gesture at this point he concluded and scurried out the back door as fast as his bullet ridden ass would take him. He waited in Fouled Anchor Alley for Maytag to appear. Bonterra would be pissed, again.

"I think that pancake syrup up his nose probably did the trick," Tombolo said to Quaid as they paid and quickly departed *Baby Rad's.*

"That was hot sauce, man." Quaid replied.

"No wonder he honked like a whale through a snorkel!"

"Yeah, whatever, I'm glad Moonbeam slowed him down," Beanne snapped.

"Who were those clowns, Bolo?" Quaid asked, "They looked like they knew you."

"They do, you just met the Little Latin asshole and the Big Fat Face pusher from last night, the dudes looking for the stones, man."

"Hoo boy!" Quaid exclaimed. He needed a break, needed time to think.

He left Beanne and Bolo to absorb their beers onboard the *Boongy,* and headed towards the *Spooner Wharf* for his favorite, early morning, let's do it all again Deep Air cocktail. Thinking came later.

DIMPLE SUE

Dimple Sue Pankersley hitched up skintight cut-offs, bent over to adjust her heel straps and checked out her new toenail paint, fluorescent emerald green. When she finished, she swung her blond-haired head like a lioness snapping a gazelle's neck and stood up. Tuesday, time for her morning shift at the *Spooner Wharf Bar* and *Institute for the Advancement of Cerebral Questing*.

Amply endowed, both fore and aft, by the creator, Dimple Sue felt the soft gums of men's hungry eyes chew her every move. She loved it. "Guys," she giggled, "who needs them, 'cept me?" She loved the tension men's eyes created, like spiders throwing hot threads of desire that suspended her on a trampoline of mistrusted, lust dusted, get busted, love. Love was a strange and confusing emotion that, in Dimple Sue's opinion, was possessed only by humans. Love is the language of a million reasons and treasons, but it's given only humans. Can that be true? She wondered if she was right.

Like most random, sensual happenings, the visual advances of a casual voyeur are safe, short and exciting. Dimple Sue knew men from chin to ankle. It was the space between their lower jaw and the upper skull that perplexed her.

The *Spooner Wharf* was aptly named because it was always crowded and patrons were forced to spoon for space at the bar.

Miss Dimple Sue Pankersley pin-balled and hip-bumped her way through the usual mixture of drunk, drunker and drunkest drunks. She toured her misty green eyes around her area of responsibility and gave an involuntary twerk. The earth stopped and several frozen drinks skidded off the bar, but Dimple Sue didn't notice, she was focused on a table near the water.

~ ~ ~

Most afternoons, when he was ashore, Quaid Butler absorbed a drink or two at the *Spooner Wharf*. He had his reasons.

Today, as usual, he occupied a table surrounded by old lobster floats near the water in Dimple Sue's area.

Every time Dimple Sue saw Quaid, she remembered the smell of the sea, warm Jack Daniels and fire on the water.

Quaid sat with the easy posture of a man who was not surprised by much. Polite, yet raunchy enough to attract her, he'd never crossed the line of propriety. Their paths intertwined a few months earlier when he came to her rescue after she burned her boyfriend's boat near Dredger's Key.

Some of Dimple Sue's waitress girlfriends said Quaid was the man who was Brandi's love in the song of the same name.

"Watch out for Quaid," one said, "you can like that guy and he won't even know it. He's somewhere else, but I hear he's a good ..."

"Drinks are up!" Tall Paul the bartender called from the bar.

Dimple Sue recalled that first evening and involuntarily started humming, *"He flies through the air with greatest of ease, the daring young man on the flying trapeze ..."*

While Quaid waited at his table, Dimple Sue hit fast forward and ran her favorite mental clip. Her good memories were few, sharp and as dense as diamonds.

Dimple Sue had no fear of, yet immense respect for, the unlimited capacity of unwise people to screw things up. She remembered her last boyfriend, Bernie, one such fool who paid the price for being stupid and not loving her right.

... By midnight she'd had enough of Bernie. He'd gone ashore and left her alone on the boat, again. That's what started it, she recalled. It was midnight, she knew this because her watch stopped after she fired a flare into the cabin of Bernie's boat and then jumped, nearly naked, into the summer sea. The fire took off much quicker than expected. There was little time to pack.

"Oops!" she laughed and shook her flooded Timex. With tits afloat in chest deep water, she stood two hundred feet away from Bernie's burning boat anchored near Dredgers Key. Her long corn-silk blond hair swept back and forth with the sea.

"Whom, I say, WHOM gives a fuck!" she bellowed, "I'm burning Bernie's boat, so what, that's funny as hell."

Sparks flew upward, like tracer rounds that crackled, died and followed other spent souls toward heaven. We're just God's bullets, she remembered thinking, used for His target practice at the stars.

Bernie had done gone and pissed her off. Sure, he'd be mad about the boat and sure she was a little impatient when it came to resolving relationship problems but then again ...

Clutching a half empty bottle of Jack Daniels she'd used the first half to start the fire, she took several hard hits. The fiery drink made her cough and snort and with each splutter she laughed and blew a gulp of booze out her nose. The liquor scorched her nostrils and felt good. The neck of Bernie's guitar, strings still attached, bobbed nearby. He'd irked her most when they went ashore and Bernie always stopped to pee on a flowering bush.

"I try to get the freaking bee's," he often told her while humming Pete Seeger's, *"Where have all the flowers gone?"*

She had to shuffle her bare feet to keep from sinking into the mud. Charred remains floated past. "FUCK YOU!" She bellowed through wet, numb lips. Fuck You, Fuck You, Fuck You. ... her words echoed off unconcerned waters. Boats and people were just snacks to mother ocean.

With mud-caked feet and a common species of Sargasso weed wedged in the crack of her ass, Dimple Sue was almost drunk, almost naked and almost happy when Quaid Butler showed up in his small boat, Sturdy, *and pulled her from the sea.*

"The fish are laughing," she'd told him with drunken seriousness.

Quaid covered her with his foul weather jacket. There were no spare clothes onboard, so he made a quick skirt out of chum bags and wrapped them around her waist. She remembered feeling and smelling like a fishing lure, but she also felt alive and free. The only "almost" still in effect was the naked part. She'd shivered with unexplained delight and offered him a swallow of her whiskey. He accepted with enthusiasm and they laughed with the fish for a long time before Quaid explained his presence.

"A taxi driver dropped some Coast Guard guy off at Trumbo Point. He saw you, in the water, actually he saw your, ah, bumpers, ah, afloat on the water, near the burning boat and called me," Quaid explained on the way back to the dock.

"Yup, tits help." Dimple took a snort, *"And unlike flares, they work better when they're wet."*

When they arrived at the Spooner Wharf *docks, Quaid refused payment and didn't try to get into her pants, not that she had any.*

"He's weird," she thought, *"I'll have to watch this one."*
Dimple Sue finished her five-second flashback and walked to Quaid's table, adjusted one hip and smiled, "Hey, Quaid Butler, how ya'll doing?"

"I'm doing well, Miss Dimple Sue, how about your own sweet selfness?"

"Yeah, I'm good, really good ... the usual?"

Quaid looked into her eyes and smiled, "In-deedy-do, Miss Dimple Sue, please oblige me with a Deep Air Daiquiri, darlin'." Dimple Sue was not surprised by the drink order; Quaid gave the bartender his Deep Air recipe a long time ago.

"You're weird, Quaid, you and this Deep Air thing. What's up with that?"

"And you, Miss Pankersley, are a rare beauty." Quaid winked and watched her blush. She flamed hot and fast like a Key West sunset.

"I think it's 'cuz your nose hairs twinkle in the sunlight," he finished.

"You numbskull!" she laughed, gave him a funny punch, then turned and when she was sure he was looking, and she *was* sure, offered her famous Jamaican Twerked Chicken dance towards the bar.

Quaid caught more women than fish. His friends said he was a chum bag for love.

Anyway, he and Beanne concocted the Deep Air Daiquiri one night, years ago, when neither could find anything that tasted good, nor tasted at all, after breathing stale, dry air for three hours during an in-water decompression.

"Paul, gimme a Deep Air for Quaid!" Dimple Sue called out.

Tall Paul, the six-foot- four-inch bartender and ex-Navy diver, limped toward the mixing station. He quickly tossed Tabasco, Mount Gay, Key Lime, draft beer and a thimble of McPherson's, *Dew of the Thistle,* into a frosty mug, poured the mixture over ice and hooked a Key West Pink shrimp on the lip.

"One Deep Air Daiquiri coming up!" Tall Paul hoisted the drink in the air, "You gotta go down, but you don't gotta come up! Right, Quaid?" Paul bellowed.

"Roger that, Navy."

Paul had danced with Deep Air once before and she'd damn near killed him.

When Dimple Sue returned with Quaid's drink, she found him hunched over on his chair with his right hand in his pocket. He seemed to be wrestling with something.

"Lonely?" Dimple Sue asked with a mischievous grin as she slowly ate his shrimp.

Quaid took his turn at the red face game, although his particular shade looked more like a baboon's ass than a Key West sunset. "No, it's my dang phone!"

"So, that's what you call it?" she grinned, turned her head and spit the shrimp tail into the water. A silver king flashed and the tail was gone.

Quaid went full baboon. Dimple Sue's shrimp lipped smile made him nervous and his hand got even further entangled.

"Let go of that thing, Quaid, it'll grow!" someone called from the raw bar. Friendly laughter echoed amid the silence of the clams. The cell phone vibrated for the last time. Quaid's nostrils flared and found Dimple Sue's scent in the wind. He quaffed the Deep Air, closed his eyes and contemplated his next move. Quaid always said, "I didn't really learn too much after thirty, just got better at being dumb."

Time, the oil that lubricates the thin interface of future and past, was running out. Civilization is like a bad paint job, Quaid thought, thick in some places, thin in others.

He checked his voice mail and found a boater was ten miles offshore and out of gas. Just another day, he thought. Quaid finished his Deep Air and stood up. It would be a short trip, but he had bills to pay.

~ ~ ~

After Quaid returned, he headed back to the *Spooner*. Within minutes Billy Beanne and Tombolo also arrived and plopped down next to him. Beanne sat under the same stinky lobster balls as before. Was it a coincidence?

"What's up boys?" Quaid asked.

"What's up is what are we going to do, Quaid? I smell a shit storm a brewin'." Beanne said.

"Do you want to die for money?" Quaid asked.

"Why the hell not, people die 'or a lot less." Tombolo quipped.

"Good point."

"Yeah, my aunt died from winning at Bingo, tits up ... heart attack, right on the 'ucking table, no shit." Bolo added.

"Good point, hum. Well, okay then, we've decided to do it, so let's do it. First, there's one thing we know that nobody else knows." Beanne and Bolo's eyes brightened.

"What's that, Quaid?"

"They don't know what we don't know."

"Huh?" Tombolo mumbled, "Listen Quaid, I'm tired o' looking into rich people's windows and dreaming. Carpets, toilets, AC units and cable! Come on boys, let's get some 'or our own-dang-selves, right Beanne?"

"That's cool Bolo," Beanne interjected, "but the more important question is not, in my unsought opinion, what we *don't* know, we all know that too well, but what we *do* know. Like, what do we know that the bad guys don't know, right?"

"Huh?" Bolo re-mumbled.

"Well put, Beanne." Sometimes, Quaid wished he had stayed in Vietnam; the rules were simpler, less confusing. "Well, we know a bunch of things, like where the *Faulty Dog* is and we know there are six full dive tanks sitting on the bottom."

"Five," said Beanne, "I used one on the de-com."

"Shit, I didn't think about the tanks. Even with 'ive there's enough air down there to go to Cuba!" Tombolo said.

"Well, we ought to have a plan then, right?" Beanne asked amid confused silence.

"Well, OK, here's *my* plan, boys," Tombolo finally offered. "You locate the short Cuban and make a deal to look 'or the stones. Tell him it's a 'ifty-'ifty split if we get them back. They'll take the deal, what other choice do they have. But, being pro'essional crooks they will want to protect their interest, so you take them to the site onboard *Betty's Boongy* to see 'or themselves. Genius, right?"

"You think they'll go for that?" Beanne asked.

"Hell, no! They'll kill you be'ore the stones dry but let me finish. Once you're on the wreck you ..."

"Heave to, Bolo, you keep saying, You, what happened to We?" Quaid asked.

"I getting to it, hold your snorkel! Anyway," Tombolo coughed and bit the filter off a Camel, which was tougher than it looked since he'd lost his front teeth. His lips held the cigarette out the side of his mouth. He lit it and went on, "you get on the wreck, find the stones then, when you're set up with the spare tanks in tow, hang a piece of coral on the anchor line so it looks like there is strain on it, then cut away the anchor. Bonterra, Naldo and Maytag go adri't but, genius here again; they won't know they're 'reaking drifting!"

'What about the *Boongy*?"

"Don't worry. They'll be scared to call the Coast Guard and eventually some 'isherman will spot them and tow the *Boongy* in. Everybody knows it's your boat, Quaid. They won't hang around long when they think someone will report you missing and, you'll make sure people see them getting on the boat be'ore you leave. It'll be *Hasta Linguini* and bye-bye."

Quaid had to admit Tombolo was pretty sharp. "Ah, I hate to sound self-absorbed, but what about me and Beanne?"

"Chill, Quaid. While you're gathering the stones, *if there are any, and incidentally, are we sure they are emeralds?* Anyway, I'll be on the way out in the small boat. You guys grab the extra tanks, ascend to about two fathoms and swim with the counter current. Come up when you get near Skinny Mon Key. I'll pick you up."

"Won't the *Boongy* drift in the same direction as me and Beanne?"

"No, Quaid, Tombolo is right." Beanne interrupted, "The prevailing wind ought to drive the boat more than the current, and *Betty's Boongy* ought to go in the opposite direction."

"You don't think they'll come after us?"

"Not when you've accidently put the keys in your vest pocket! They'll probably think you're dead when you don't come up in an hour or so. They'll keep looking for you, not knowing they are floating away. Genius plan, 'unny as hell right, huh? And anyway, would you stay in town when the *word* gets out that two local guys are missing and were last seen in the company o' a really big Samoan and a suspicious Spaniard?" Bolo asked.

"Yeah, Beanne inserted, "the cops ought to put them in the Witless Protection program!"

"Funny, Beanne. You know you might be right, Bolo, but how does the "word" get out?"

"Simple ... Dimple." Bolo said.

Tombolo's buoyant intellect must have germinated when evolution stopped to take a whiz, Quaid thought, but he did have some good ideas.

~ ~ ~

The *Spooner Wharf Bar* was as full as Dimple Sue's tank top when she arrived for her night shift. She'd been working doubles to save money for a trip. The words, "Spoon at the Spooner" were printed in fluorescent pink, shrimp-shaped letters on the front. The S's were almost worn off from pushing her way through patrons.

Beanne and Tombolo liked Dimple Sue and smiled when she arrived at the table. She leaned over; pencil poised, cocked her head and waited.

"We'll have two of whatever Quaid is having," Beanne said, slowly forcing his eyes to look at hers. Two was the only number he could think of. Tombolo took advantage of the cover and plunged eyeball first into the mythical cleavage.

"Two more Deep Airs, Paul," Dimple Sue called towards the bar.

"Coming up," Paul laughed and noticed Tombolo's hypnotic state. He got Bolo's attention and put his fist on top of his head. It was the international divers signal for, "Are you OK?" Tombolo tore his eyes away and returned the signal.

~ ~ ~

Just before closing, a drunk slipped off his stool and joined other pickled pilgrims at the under-bar, a habitation he would occupy until the cleaning service arrived at four a.m. and removed the remnants of yesterday's reality.

Night blooming jasmine, stale beer and dead bait tinctured the air while non-perishable plastic floated along the seawall waiting to be carried northward by the

Gulfstream into the gyre of the Sargasso Sea and onward toward the Great North Atlantic Garbage Patch.

"LAST CALL!" Dimple Sue bellowed and waited until the remaining un-hidden pilgrim was dragged from the bar. She found herself thinking about the parallel grooves in the dirt his dragging flip-flops carved out. Good furrow for beans, she thought and took a second to remember her days on the family farm in Odessa, Texas, where she'd learned that horses, hunks and hot sauce were all any woman really needed to get along except, of course, for sparkling stones and shiny gold. You could get too much of the first three, but never enough of the last two.

Quaid signaled for one more round. She got their drinks and with softer eyes, she came to the table and looked at Quaid. "What's this all about, boys?" Dimple Sue drew her apron away like a bullfighter's cape to reveal legs that carried a dream.

"Well, Miss Dimple Sue," Quaid coughed to snap Bolo and Beanne out of their trance, "ah, we have a little situation that you might be able to help us with."

"What's that ... never mind ... don't tell me... you're broke?" she smiled.

"No, it's nothing like that. Do you remember seeing a great big Samoanish-looking guy with a little Cubanish-looking guy recently?"

"Yeah, oh hell yeah, I remember that circus act. They came in here a few days ago looking for someone ... was it you, Quaid?"

"Ah, what did they say?"

"Didn't really say much, just they were looking for some assholes. There were plenty to pick from but they sat down anyway, had a few drinks, looked around and then... all hell broke loose."

"What do you mean?"

"Well, the big one drank six Mai Tai's, umbrella's and all, real fast, then got up to leave and leaned against Tall Paul's van to prevent falling down. He tipped it over."

"That must've pissed Paul off."

"No shit, it landed on Lady Barfly, his dog, crushed her flat and then the fat dude walked away without so much as a howdy-do."

"How's the dog doing?' Tombolo asked.

"Not so good, I hear she's still dead."

"Anyway Dimple Sue," Quaid interrupted, "to answer your question, yes, it might've been me they were looking for."

"What did you do, Quaid?"

"Well, it's a long story."

"Yeah, it's a long story," Bolo and Beanne chimed.

"Well, look boys, we're on the other side of sunrise now and we got plenty time and plenty ice."

Dimple Sue headed for the bar. She knew men can be messy, but fun, and she smelled a wild storm a-brewing. "It's all about fun, ain't it," she remarked to a stack of damp napkins and poured a double Deep Air for herself.

"That's some wild woman there, Quaid." Beanne nodded.

"Yeah, Beanne, and we're about to find out just how wild she is."

Dimple Sue returned with their drinks and slid them across the guano specked table. Three thirsty men tossed them back then looked at Dimple Sue.

Quaid began. "Bolo, tell her your idea. ... Never mind, I guess I should tell her why we need to tell her your idea. Maybe I'll start at the beginning."

"Good idea." Dimple Sue grinned.

"Well, it started with a call from Cole Shaw, a local insurance agent."

"Yeah, I know Cole. He comes in here and sucks pimentos out of the olives when he thinks no one is looking."

"Ah, okay, anyway a few days ago somebody's boat sank out near Skinny Mon Key. It was called the *Faulty Dog*."

"Yeah, I know the boat," Dimple Sue said, "belongs to old man Morley, the Fire Ant, right?"

"Yep, that's right," Quaid said.

"He sold it again?"

"Yup, he sold her to a guy named McCreedy. Anyway, Cole's company insured the boat and he wanted us to go out and find it. He thought it might be a deliberate scuttle job, so we did. I got Beanne and Bolo here and we went down and found it in 206 feet of water off Skinny Mon Key. I went inside the boat to find why it sank and ..." Quaid went on to tell the tale. It took ten minutes before he got to the part involving Dimple Sue.

"So, Dimple Sue ... Sue ..." Quaid got so wrapped up in his story he hadn't noticed Dimple Sue nodding off. She'd been on her feet for two back-to-back shifts, Quaid remembered and Beanne and Bolo were too polite to say anything.

"Let's try again tomorrow." Quaid said and gently poked Dimple Sue.

"So," she stretched with a sleepy smile, "If it wasn't for Moonbeam you'd be screwed, right? Are we there yet?"

"Dimple Sue, you are some wild thang," Tombolo said.

"I didn't get here by crying for what I want."

Quaid helped Dimple Sue back to her apartment, tucked her in and wondered if he'd pulled the blanket up high enough.

The next morning, they met onboard the *Boongy*. Tombolo's plan was explained again to Dimple Sue who said she had a dream about it and, of course, agreed to help. "How much you think these *maybe* emeralds are worth, Quaid?" She asked.

"Judging by the way those guys are chasing after us it must be a lot. We need to find out who these guys are; we don't even know their names." Quaid noted.

"A lot, like a lot of money, like enough to buy an Airstream with a composting toilet?"

"Yeah, probably."

"OK, boys, I'm in." With a quick spin on a three-inch heel, she headed for the Spooner watching for cracks between the boards.

After Paul scraped his dog off the sidewalk in front of the *Spooner Wharf*, he'd made it his business to find the overblown Samoan and his Christmas ornament-sized pal.

Tall Paul was hosing the bar down when Dimple Sue walked in and told him what she needed.

"Their names are Maytag and Naldo." Paul said, "Made is my bidness to find them fucks. Maytag is the big one who tipped my camper over on Lady Barfly, I love her, I ..."

"I know, Paul, I know. How's she doing?" Sue asked.

"Not so good. She ain't come back to life yet. Even used the vacuum on her ..."

"Oh, sorry Paul, keep praying, maybe change accessories."

"Thanks," Paul said. He went on to report that Maytag and Naldo were staying nearby, at the Gripps Hotel.

"Thanks big guy, I owe you one," Dimple Sue said when he finished. She winked at him and spun on her heel. She was good at it, called it her "Signature Move."

"Once I find my gun," Paul swore to Dimple Sue's naturally twerking backside, "I'm gonna come to Gripps with it and shoot that Samoan dough boy!"

Dimple Sue moved away and nodded backwards with a smile. Some folks are just born to twerk.

"Debt paid," Tall Paul said quietly with a grin.

~ ~ ~

Onboard *Betty's Boongy*, Quaid, Beanne and Bolo squatted ass down on the deck like captured Viet Cong. They were roasting Vienna sausages and marshmallows over a can of Sterno when Dimple Sue returned and told them that, thanks to Paul, she knew not only the bad guys names, but where they were staying.

"Do you think it could involve drugs, Quaid?" she asked.

"What doesn't?"

"Well, who's going to go and shake up the little punk Naldo?" Bolo asked.

"I think we should all go," Quaid said. "If things go south it's going to take at least three of us to handle Maytag. That leaves Dimple Sue to handle Naldo."

"Think you can whup him, Dimple Sue?" Bolo prodded.

"Hell yes, I trained Moonbeam, plus you boys know what I'm capable of, or at least you like to think about it, don't cha?"

"Yes, ma'am," they grinned and looked at her feet.

"Nice nail polish, Dimple Sue." Bolo remarked.

"And anyway, things can't *go south*, man. We're already at the Southernmost Point." Beanne noted.

"OK, listen to me boys, if you want this thing to work, here's what we gotta do." Dimple Sue looked around and then explained.

FOWL ODOR

The hotel suite shrank like a condom in the sun as Senor Ignacio Bonterra paced the floor in front of Maytag and Naldo. The stench of his cheap cigar and other mysterious nostrilic invaders reminded Naldo of a Cuban goat fart. He missed the old country.

Maytag, on the other hand, was hungry and reached across the desk for a little pink pencil eraser. Bonterra slapped his wrist. It felt like spanking a ham.

"Let me see if I understand the situation. McCreedy is gone; probably back to Canada, Sí?"

"Sí." Maytag and Naldo nodded meekly.

"And, Maytag had his ass kicked by a waitress named Moonbeam, Sí?"

"Sí."

"And, we are no closer to finding dee stones now than we were a few days ago, Sí?"

"Sí."

"Are you sure one of those bullets didn't hit the cord from your ass to your brain?" Bonterra eyeballed Naldo.

"Sí?"

"All right, here's what we are going to..."

There was a knock at the entrance. Bonterra reached for his gun. Maytag waddled to the door and peeked through the peephole.

"Is woman."

Bonterra nodded. Maytag pulled the door handle violently. Unfortunately, the door was designed to open outwards. The doorknob and lock tore out, hit Maytag in the face and sent him reeling across the room where he landed on a couch that collapsed like a cheap minivan. Dimple Sue, impatient as always, pulled the remnants of the door open, pushed Naldo aside and walked in.

"Oh, hi boys! My name is Dimple Sue. So there are three of you, huh? I was wondering. Anyway, I'm here to help solve a problem."

Dimple Sue was taller than Bonterra and Naldo. It took several seconds and a lot of effort for them to raise their eyes from her tank top to her face.

"Please come in." Bonterra pulled his gun and pointed it at her. "What is this problem you will solve for us, *Chica*?"

"The problem of you staying alive if you don't find the missing stones, I think they're emeralds ... right?"

Bonterra, Naldo and even Maytag from the floor, stole quick glances at each other.

"Who are you and what you can do for us?"

"I told you fuzz nuts, I'm Dimple Sue Pankersley." She walked toward Bonterra until her cotton-covered nipples were in line with the gun barrel, dipped, took one step closer and nestled the cold blue steel between her breasts. She stood tall, pushed herself together with her elbows, and the gun disappeared. It was a trick that has fascinated men for eons. The barrel would leave an oily stain on her crenulated tank top but it was worth the effect.

"I'm friends with the guys you are trying to chase down to find the stones. They're emeralds, right? Here's how it's going to work ..."

Bonterra could no longer see his gun, although he looked intensely.

"Are you, young girl with big casabas, telling me, old man with big gun how eet's going to work?" Bonterra tried to look up.

"Yup, afraid so, *Seenyor Boner.*" Dimple Sue looked down into his red-rimmed eyes. "Think about it, amigo, you don't have a choice, but there is one good decision you can make right now so you won't feel too stupid..."

"And what is that?" Bonterra asked, tugging gently on the pistol grip. His fingers were going numb.

"You can decide to sit down, shut up and listen to me." Dimple Sue was on a roll. She hadn't had this much fun since burning Bernie's boat. Dimple Sue dropped her elbows and stepped back. The gun magically appeared and she stuck one of her well-manicured, emerald colored fingernails into the barrel.

Bonterra's double chin trembled as one and his anger at Dimple Sue's unabashed cheekiness flushed his corpulent face. Bonterra went full baboon and looked like a steamed red beet with ears and pointy shoes.

"Sit down, before I blow you down," Dimple Sue said with vegetarian pleasantness and adjusted her tank top with her free hand. "Breathe everyone, breathe, breathe ..."

The trio of criminals looked up like hungry koi at feeding time. Before they could close their mouths, or sit down, Dimple Sue instructed them to be at the *Spooner Wharf* around nine o'clock that night. "Come alone," she said, "except for each other, understood?" She pulled her finger out of the gun barrel with a popping sound and blew on it. "We'll figure this thing out, OK?"

"Sí," Bonterra hissed.

"Sí," Naldo muttered.

Dimple Sue glanced at Maytag, "Do I need to bring Moonbeam?"

"*Alu ese ma a'u!*" (Leave me alone!) Maytag thrashed half-heartedly amid the crumpled ruins.

Dimple Sue's laser smile caught each man full in the fac like a spotlight in a cop show. She pushed the damaged doo open with her butt, spun on one heel and walked away.

It took both men to pry Maytag from the wreckage.

By eight o'clock that night, Bonterra had contacted hi "Peeples" in Miami, been verbally abused, threatened witl public dismemberment and ordered to, "Get the freaking stone back." And among warnings regarding any future screw-ups, i was agreed that once the stones were in Bonterra's hands, Quaid Beanne and Tombolo would be free to leave, just not alive.

BOBBING SAMOAN

Seven uncertain idiots met that night at the *Spooner Wharf*. Everyone took a chair except Maytag who, too large to fit, chose to lean against the weathered wooden railing. He looked like a combination of Humphrey Bogart and a medicine ball. The railing, built to withstand drunks up to 45 MPH, could not withstand the giant Samoan. Sun baked wood splintered, rusty fasteners failed and Maytag plunged into the oily harbor water.

The usual group of curious drunks ambled over to the bulkhead to take a whiz and see what was going on. Maytag scratched and clawed his way along the concrete wall and instinctively attempted to avoid the fate of other flotsam destined for the Great Garbage Patch in the North Atlantic. Quaid coached Maytag, "Swim or die, swim or die..." but the big one was fading fast. He could float but not swim and his center of gravity was so low and he couldn't roll onto his back.

Eventually, a fisherman bagged Maytag's head with a fish net, to keep his face out of the water, while another back country guide used a push pole to prod him along the bulkhead towards a ladder.

Silently, with little fanfare and only a few stinky bubbles, a bull manatee surfaced behind Maytag. The mammal's two watertight nostrils vented in lustful desire and Quaid noticed it had strange looking miniature antennae on its ass.

"Vili le leoleo!" (Call the police!) Maytag yelled as the manatee attempted to mount him and begin the

79

predictable and perfectly natural mating ritual. The pair looked like sponge cakes in heat. Maytag was unusually passive during the initial advances. The process, not long, complicated or pretty is not worth repeating. Dimple Sue finally drove the lustful manatee away by leaning over the bulkhead, distracting it with her cleavage and sticking heads of rotted lettuce in its up turned nostrils.

Fifteen drunks, working in friendly discord, hauled Maytag out of the water, onto the dock and hosed him off. Then the meeting began in earnest.

While Maytag, who would eventually require multi-specie sex counseling, drip-dried on the dock, the requisite insults, threats and intimidations were uttered and re-uttered until their stench hung in the air like an old shrimp net, but an agreement between the parties was finally reached.

~ ~ ~

It would take most of the next day to outfit *Betty's Boongy* for a second dive. Quaid was confident he could find the wreck again since both he and Tombolo took numerous GPS readings when anchored on the site.

Two days later, *Betty's Boongy* slipped her lines and headed for the reef. On board were Quaid, Beanne, Maytag, Naldo and Bonterra.

"Where is woman, she not to be making dee swimming an' dee tanning of all dee places?" Naldo asked.

"Nope, Dimple Sue had to work." Quaid replied

"Oh, is sad for my eyes not to not see. "

"Where is one Tombolo?" Bonterra asked.

"He had a dentist appointment."

"For teeth?"

"Yes."

"Gap?"

"Yes, Sí."

This information seemed to both satisfy and pique Bonterra's curiosity as they a motored southward. No one had much to say. *Betty's Boongy* rolled cheek to cheek in the soft beam sea. Each soul on board smiled politely while each tried to figure out how to screw the other. They had reserved no time for pleasant conversation.

From Bonterra's point of view it was simple. He had the gun, or Naldo did, so he had the boat. Even with *"fleepers"* the chances of Quaid and Beanne swimming to shore were slim. When they came up with the stones, Maytag would grab the bag, Naldo would shoot them in the top of the head and Bonterra would set them free then return to shore, run the boat up on the beach and haul ass.

In the cabin, the noise of the diesel engine made it difficult for Bonterra to overhear Quaid and Beanne.

"Well, here we go," Quaid said, "I was hoping the wind would be a little more out of the North."

"Don't worry; it won't be a problem unless the wind goes solid East."

"Roger that."

It took an hour and a half to reach the wreck site. Quaid did a grid search with his video fish finder and marked the sailboat several times. They slowly dragged a grapnel hook 10 feet off the bottom. The third time they passed directly over the wreck the hook snagged in the rigging. A small bungee cord, attached to the main anchor line, was designed to fail and absorbed the shock. Before the bungee snapped, Quaid cut the engine. The coiled anchor line paid out then came tight. What luck, they'd hooked the rigging a second time!

Once geared up, Beanne felt he ought to explain the dive plan and told Bonterra he ought to expect them back within an hour. Quaid and Beanne final-checked each other's gear, "That ought to do it," Beanne said. Quaid grinned; at least Beanne's oughtism went away under water.

Naldo was excited; it was his first time at sea. He waved enthusiastically at the divers. His gun fell out of his waistband, hit the deck and discharged. Quaid and Beanne pretended not to notice and fell backwards into the sea. Two streams of silver bubbles disappeared into the welcoming blue. Sea and wind were the same as before and at ninety feet a familiar rapture embraced their eager brains, like hot sauce on an oyster. The water wrapped like swaddling cloth and Beanne hungered for red jellybeans.

However, since this could be considered a life or death situation, Quaid and Beanne decided to cut out any antics and agreed to remain straight throughout the dive. It was a futile gesture.

At 90 feet, the Rapture of the Deep encouraged them like a first kiss. The *Salty Dog* sat upright as before, her mainsail flapped contentedly, like an old horsetail in fly season. The diffused light dimmed as a cloud passed overhead.

"Urgle gurgle burgle!" (*Wait a minute!*) Quaid burbled and pointed to the mast 30 feet below. There, tangled ass up in the spreaders, with shrunken arms outstretched, was *Conchita*. Apparently Tombolo's jabs with the boat hook were lethal and sufficient to deflate the doll. He guessed the voice simulator, battery, nitrous oxide cartridge and the stones made her heavy enough to sink straight down.

Quaid and Beanne swam toward *Conchita* and carefully untangled the slime-covered plastic. Quaid noticed the doll's feet had sand in the bottom like the old Bobo the Clown blow-up punching bag. Apparently, like Bobo and bad politicians, she always bounced back.

Quaid located the Special Projects area, found the slimy Kevlar pouch, took a peek inside and gave Beanne the thumbs up. "Yurgle Hurgle!" Quaid unzipped the top part of his wet suit and carefully tucked the slippery bag into his Speedo.

Meanwhile, Beanne rolled *Conchita* into a tight wad and lashed her to the mast with her own fish net stockings. The saying, *"Hung by his own petard,"* came to mind.

Sadly, she presented a less dramatic image than Captain Ahab lashed to Moby Dick's harpooned body and really, this was neither the time nor place for inflatable emotions or literary comparisons.

Strung out on the sandy bottom the five full dive tanks from the previous dive sat ready to go. Beanne grinned, Quaid laughed, they both choked.

"Urgle!" Quaid burbled. Beanne nodded and finished his descent to the sandy bottom. He swam with his head down to avoid stirring the sand around the wreck and looked for any loose stones. Off to his right he noticed a glint of light and found a stone crab sitting on top of a stone in its shallow sand nest. The stone crab wasn't stoned, but Beanne was, and drew his dive knife. He teased the crab into grabbing the blade and reached for the abandoned stone. The crab, on the other hand, decided to go for something more palatable. He let go of the knife and clamped on to Beanne's Achilles tendon just above his flipper strap. "Urgle Urglee!"

Beanne kicked at the ill-mannered crustacean and ascended to the masthead. When he looked down the crab was gone but its claw was still clamped on his tendon. He reached down, pulled it free and stuffed it down the front his Speedo, dinner he thought. The claw finished clamping, "Furgleeee!"

At two hundred six feet, with three minutes of bottom time, Quaid untied the spare tanks and bundled them into two sets. Each tank had its own regulator so an in-water change out, a dangerous stunt at best, would not be necessary. He also tied a piece of dead coral onto the *Boongy's* anchor line and with a nod at Beanne, cut the anchor free. Quaid and Beanne checked their compasses and began a controlled ascent toward the counter current that flowed, like back spin on a Q-ball, west along the face of the reef, toward Skinny Mon Key. They had plenty of time, and air to, decompress and *"bulrgle shirgle"* along the way.

~ ~ ~

Bobbing on the *Boongy*, Bonterra, Naldo and Maytag waited patiently for the divers to surface. After half an hour, Maytag asked, *"O fea le fale ta'ele?* (Where is the toilet?) Bonterra pointed at the ever changing sea. Maytag reached for his crotch and headed for the rail where his weight, combined with an unexpected swell, caused *Betty's Boongy* to roll heavily to the port side.

Maytag went overboard still looking for his *Poki*. Bonterra slid sideways and hit the cabin wall face first where he was joined by Naldo who slammed ass first into a fire extinguisher. Bonterra cursed like a mad man, Naldo checked his butt and Maytag kept a sharp eye out for manatees.

With a 300-pound Samoan over the side, the divers being gone for almost an hour and no clue what to do next, the gangsters admittedly had a problem.

If viewed from above, the boat with Maytag alongside looked like a miniature version of a Japanese whaling ship preparing to flense out a big humpback somewhere in the North Atlantic. Maytag flailed wildly at first, an honorable but futile gesture. It soon became obvious they would have to tow Maytag back to shore. Maytag did not seem comfortable with this idea and continued floundering alongside the boat. Bonterra paced the deck like Captain Bligh in a cheap leisure suit. Occasionally, Naldo could see Maytag's nose and frightened eyes pop up above the gunwale as he made heroic attempts to heave himself back into the boat. At least he's on his back; Naldo thought and threw a fender over the side for Maytag to hold onto. Curious schooling fish gathered around below the Samoan. A fast barracuda flashed then stopped, holding motionless a silent sentinel below the iceberg ass.

Maytag's noisy insistence on survival began to annoy Bonterra. He moved forward into the cabin and stuffed wads of paper into his ears. It was pink and smelled bad but was necessary. A moaning Samoan is not known to be a particularly melodic source of musical expression.

The sky grew darker, and the wind changed direction. Grey clouds, like old winos, shuffled in from the east.

Bonterra pinched the bridge of his nose and sat quietly. After a few moments he turned to Naldo, "We must go, Naldy, we must leave this place."

Alongside, Maytag scuffled even more violently. He knew he was expendable but still ...

"Ugga, ugga, ook ook!" (No translation available.) He cried to no avail.

Bonterra nodded toward the gunwale, "Fuck heem."

He walked aft and without warning punched Naldo in the nose. The blood flow was immediate and abundant. Bonterra dragged Naldo to the rail by the scruff of his neck and squeezed his head. Fresh Naldo blood mixed with the water surrounding Maytag. The schools of fish grew large, fast.

Bonterra had never been fond of the looming Maytag anyway, so there was no point in dragging this out. "If I let the sharks do their work there will be one less fool to worry about," Bonterra said in way of explanation to Naldo. "Cut Maytag loose, untie the anchor rope and start the engine, Naldy."

Naldo moved to the helm station, and looked around. "Dee key is not to be founded." Naldo said.

"Fuck!"

Bonterra raised his hands in supplication and recalled an old pirate dirge. He went to the rail and repeated it above Maytag's head like a prayer,

"The only man you can trust is a dead man, for it's he who'll tell no tales. No? Si? Get it?"

Maytag, however, was not interested in old white pirate tales and dredged up a saying that his people, who had lived in harmony with the sea for thousands of years used frequently and sincerely, *"Out e le malamalama,"* (I don't understand.)

Maytag, a fun-loving Samoan, found the lack of humor during this entire misadventure involving skinny white guys and aggressive mammals irked him. Samoans do not take to being irked and Maytag had never been this irked before. He'd rather be home, squatting in the sand, pounding on a coconut with a rock and far away from all the white man's irksome irkings.

He reached deep into his ancestral Samoan soul and mustered every bit of native energy to climb onboard. It didn't help, but on the bright side, the surface suction from the drifting *Boongy* kept him alongside. Naldo didn't have the heart to poke at him with a stick.

Bonterra assumed Maytag would drift away in the bloody water. No one realized they'd already been adrift for over 40 minutes, nor did anyone including Quaid and Beanne, notice the wind change to the east or that *Betty's Boongy,* with Maytag bobbing alongside, was now headed in the same direction as Quaid and Beanne.

Betty's Boongy, blown by a fickle wind, drifted slowly toward the unforgiving coral teeth of the Skinny Mon.

THE RECSUE

Ashore, Tombolo made a final check of the small boat and tossed her mooring lines on the dock. The motor vessel, STURDY, (the painted *S* was nearly worn off from rubbing on a fender,) was an ex-Coast Guard inflatable patrol craft, capable, dependable and fast. If the weather held, it should take less than 30 minutes to reach Skinny Mon Key and locate Quaid and Beanne.

As Bolo approached Skinny Mon, he noticed a vessel silhouetted offshore in the general area where he expected to find his pals. Sensing something awry, Tombolo stood to get a better view, tripped and ripped the fuel hose off the engine, destroying the delicate coupling.

"Oh ... 'uck and double ... 'uck!" Bolo bawled across the soundless sea.

Standing upright, he saw the boat was indeed *Betty's Boongy*. That meant the *Boongy* and the boys below were drifting towards the same point. Bolo tried every trick in the book to reconnect the gas line but was unsuccessful. The remaining gas in the hose drained into the bilge, vapors billowed and the outgoing tide swept the helpless *Sturdy* toward Skinny Mon Key.

Not into futile gestures, Tombolo kicked back, bit the filter off a Camel, spit it overboard and lit up. "This ain't my first ro ..."

~ ~ ~

"*Madre de Fumar*, what eez deez?" Naldo squinted, and pointed at a smoky fireball north of Skinny Mon Key.

~ ~ ~

After being blown overboard, Tombolo struggled to the surface in time to witness the gas tank explode and *Sturdy* go bow up and sink with a sizzle in the sea. The stench of burning rubber and his own singed ponytail were almost unbearable, but overall he was OK. He rotated while he treaded water, his smelly ponytail teased like a marlin lure. Bolo's only companion was the Camel filter he'd so casually bitten off and spewn overboard. Its short virgin whiteness floated just out of reach and already attracted the attention of small fish, then larger.

Damn filter will probably outlive me, he caught himself thinking. Tombolo looked around. "I'm bait," he said quietly, "and someday we'll all be bones."

Quaid and Beanne checked their wrist compasses and ascended slowly near Skinny Mon Key. Beanne noticed a shadow on the bottom as they ascended but forgot about it as the reef came into view. Anxious to know their location, Quaid and Beanne popped to the surface and found themselves staring at the starboard side of *Betty's Boongy* 100 yards away. She'd drifted along the same course they swam. Damn east wind.

It was the boat's hull that created the shadow overhead, Beanne realized. I ought to look up next time, I ought to have known better, I ...

Betty's Boongy drifted towards the reef. If Quaid and Beanne could get close enough to climb onboard, Bonterra would kill them. On the other hand, if Bonterra didn't let them onboard, he, Naldo and Maytag, might also die as the boat pounded itself to pieces on Skinny Mon Reef.

A bedraggled Tombolo hauled himself out of the water and crawled up behind a small sand berm on the north side of Skinny Mon Key. Hidden by a dry hump between two wet spots, an irony that did not escape him, he observed a life and death scene played out just offshore. The Samoan appeared to be in the water alongside the *Boongy*. Bolo hoped Quaid could convince Bonterra to work with them, at least until they got back to shore. He pondered the situation for a moment then slipped ass first into the briny.

Skinny Mon Key

In the lee of the island, wind combined with tidal current and *Betty's Boongy* began to accelerate towards Quaid and Beanne. The exhausted divers swam for shore. When Quaid looked back he noticed *Betty's Boongy* had stopped drifting. The piece of coral tied on the anchor line must've wedged in the bottom! *Betty's Boongy* swung into the wind. They spotted Maytag. At the same time Naldo and Bonterra spotted them. Damn!

It was a standoff. Bonterra had the gun and boat, Quaid had the stones and an urge to pee.

DON'T EVER GIVE UP

Onboard *Betty's Boongy*, Bonterra turned away from a poster hanging on the bulkhead. His response to the sighting was short and to the point.

"Shoot them, Naldy! Keel heem for dee stones!"

"Sí, Senor Bonterra, wheech one?"

"What do you mean, wheech one?"

"Senor, I am most sad to say I have only one bullet left. Dee other bullet shot itself, remember, *sí*, no?"

Bonterra sighed deeply. "And why, Naldy, did you have only two bullets to begin with?"

"*Porque* only two bullet in dee gun when you geeve heem to me to keel Deek, Señor Bonterra."

Bonterra suffered a troubling memory of his stint on the toilet at the Gripps. His polyester suit grew granny girdle tight and his breath farted out in short spasmodic gasps. He was losing his grip on reality.

"You, you, you, you ... *Ah, Madre de Richardo Cabeza!* Oh well," he looked sideways at Naldo, popped a handful of Tums and two Xanex, "at least one bullet is left to keel Maytag," Bonterra elbowed Naldo in the ribs. "All it takes is one bullet, right Naldy?"

Naldo shuddered; he hated being elbowed almost as much as he hated being called Naldy. "Sí, Senor, only one."

"*Ua 'ou ma'alili.*" (I'm cold.) Maytag splashed in futile splendor.

"Shut dee fuck up!" Bonterra croaked.

Earlier, Bonterra had tried to hotwire the starter but was uncomfortable hanging upside down in a 120° engine compartment working with old electrical wires and diesel vapor. He got sea sick, and before he could get out of the engine space, puked up his nose. It put him in a foul mood. Naldo didn't have a clue and the bobbing Maytag was not much use. However, in the name of survival and good manners perhaps a solution could be worked out, and although Bonterra would not accept a defeat himself, he could easily accept it in others.

While the exhausted divers flippered toward the beach, Tombolo breaststroked out and around the front of the reef towards *Betty's Boongy*. His pony tail snagged some Sargasso seaweed and with only his eyes and nose above the surface he looked like one of a million other globs of flotsam on the sea, like an albino sea turtle with a bad hair piece.

Tombolo knew the sea, he was born at sea. His mother gave birth to him during a stormy fishing trip onboard an old wooden head boat out of Nags Head, North Carolina. His umbilical cord was severed with a filet knife and tied off with monofilament fishing line. Hosed off, swaddled in old bait net, he was given a red cork bobber to chew on and carried ashore where his mom hung him from a fish rack while she dug through her purse for car keys and cigarettes.

~ ~ ~

Quaid and Beanne reached the shoreline, took off their gear and started searching for Tombolo and *Sturdy*.

Offshore, Tombolo looked back to see them wandering around the island. He said nothing as he swam alongside *Betty's Boongy* where Maytag floated with hereditary buoyancy. In fact, the Samoan appeared to be asleep, floating on his back. Tombolo slipped his canvas belt around one of Maytag's wrists and quietly paddled away with the goliath in tow. Bonterra and Naldo were busy watching Quaid and Beanne on the beach and didn't notice Maytag's absence.

Bolo had a hostage.

More than halfway back to shore, Maytag awoke with a start and decided to change positions. He almost drowned. Tombolo rolled Maytag back and forth building momentum then flipped him over, like a beetle on its back. The sodden Samoan seemed grateful and mumbled, *"Fa'afetai,"*

Now that the sun was behind them, Quaid and Beanne spotted Tombolo and Maytag heading for shore. So did Bonterra and Naldo.

"What the hell is Tombolo doing with Maytag?" Beanne asked.

"Beats me, Beanne"

Within a few minutes Tombolo made it to the beach. They hauled Maytag out of the water, above the high tide line. His Samoan buttocks left a broad gulley in the sand. Good furrow for beans, Quaid caught himself thinking.

~ ~ ~

Squatting behind the sandy berm and hopefully out of gun range, they tried to calculate their next move. Tired, hungry, thirsty and alone on a deserted island without a Tiki bar, the situation did not seem promising.

"Bolo, what in the hell are you doing with Maytag and where is *Sturdy*?" Quaid chewed on a piece of Sargasso weed for nourishment.

"The *Sturdy* burnt up, POOF! Sorry, and then I took this clown as a hostage, man. It's the newest thing."

"I see that, but what are you going to do with him? He's too big to put on a stick and hold over a fire." Quaid said, suddenly feeling nauseous.

"What happened to *we*?" Bolo fired back. "Anyway, I was thinking that maybe *we* drag Maytag out on the beach and pretend to beat the shit out of him until Bonterra agrees to throw the gun overboard. Then we figure this out, without hurting anyone's feelings or bodies."

Resembling three sand-covered dung beetles, the trio managed to roll Maytag up the mound and into a clear spot on the small beach, visible from *Betty's Boongy*. Maytag was awake but did not put up much resistance. At one point he said, "*O le gagana e tasi e le lava!*" No one knew what it meant, but he seemed calm and ready to meet his fate.

"Ahoy, Senor Bonterra! Let's have a friendly talk or we will kill Maytag!" Quaid's voice traveled as quickly as the smell of undigested Sargasso weed and bounced hard off soft water.

"Fuck heem!" Bonterra called back, followed by a clear and present finger signal. "Bring the stones to me and take us back to shore or else!"

The words, "or else," lingered in the salted air.

Maytag's basic understanding of English, especially the phrase, "Fuck heem," allowed him to grasp Bonterra's meaning and more importantly, his intent. Maytag was, after all, a Samoan with pure Polynesian feelings and to be abandoned by one to whom he was loyal for money, of course, did not sit well with the big fella.

"I will help you." Maytag whispered to Tombolo and gave him a hug. Bolo disappeared into the fleshy mass for a moment then returned.

"Grassy-ass," the red faced Bolo said, stunned that Maytag spoke English. He went to search the beach for lethal looking conch shells.

When he returned, Tombolo slipped a pair of Queen Conch shells over his hands like huge brass knuckles and pretended to beat the shit out of the supine Maytag. Maytag, for his part, went along with the ruse for a while. His painful cries and unique brand of Samoan moaning were overheard by the frigate birds circling 1000 feet above. When Maytag tired of shrieking and groaning, Tombolo took over. The birds left.

Naldo also saw the large birds overhead and thought they were buzzards, a bad omen.

Finally, Naldo could bear no more screams of pain. Maytag was a good guy and did not deserve to be beaten to death with tourist gifts. Without hesitation, Naldo pulled his gun and moved to stand behind Bonterra who was taking a whiz over the same side where Maytag had been. He silently mimicked Bonterra's recent words, "One bullet is enough right, *NALDY*?" and squeezed. The projectile exited Bonterra's right eye socket and plopped into the shallow water near the beach. Minnows schooled around the bloody slug. The bullet's impact knocked Bonterra overboard. For *heem*, the light was forever gone.

"I never be called *Naldy* again!" he cried at Bonterra's bobbing body then held the gun in the air for Quaid to see and dramatically tossed it into the reddening water.

Naldo watched long enough to see a barracuda knock its front teeth out when it mistook the glinting steel for a fresh ballyhoo. It was cocktail hour on the reef and hors d'oeuvres were served.

Naldo soon tired of watching Bonterra's body being jerked offshore by frenetic reef sharks and turned his attention to the beach.

"*Haloo*, peoples in dee sand," he called, "Eez me, Naldo. Please stop to make poundings on dee Maytag."

Tombolo ceased pretending to pummel Maytag and gently awoke him. Apparently, he was comfortable in the sand and had fallen asleep.

"*Haloo* to you." Quaid called back across the water.

"You see me? I throw gun into water."

"Yeah, I also see you throw Bonterra into water."

"No senor, dee bullet push heem, dee bullet, no me. He only gives me two! *Conjo!*" Naldo, an unwitting disciple of Darwin, went on. "Senor Bonterra is of no meaning now, only for food, but we must go down to beezness, to make surviving of dee fattest."

Quaid looked at Beanne, Bolo and Maytag, everyone was exhausted and it was well past beer-thirty. "Okay, Naldo, let's talk."

Quaid and Beanne swam out to the boat. Naldo looked deflated as they climbed onboard. He simply wanted to get ashore, alive.

The immediate problem was getting Maytag back onboard.

While Quaid started the engine, Beanne recovered the anchor line and untied the piece of coral. Quaid motored nearer to the beach. Tombolo dug out the spare anchor and connected it to the anchor line. Beanne jumped overboard and dragged the anchor and line ashore and buried it deep in the sand and coral. Quaid backed toward the beach while Tombolo worked the deck and pulled the slack out of the anchor line. When he was as close as possible, Bolo tied off the anchor line and Quaid pulled forward, away from the beach and against the anchor. The prop wash excavated the sand behind *Betty's Boongy*. Quaid slowly maneuvered closer and eventually got near enough to the beach for them to haul Maytag onboard, and when he landed on the deck, Quaid swore he heard him say, "Moonbeam ..."

Quaid hoped the Marine Patrol would not spot them and think they were kidnapping a manatee. Eager sand filled the dredge hole as *Betty's Boongy* motored away. There was no sign anyone had been there except for two abandoned conch shells lying side by side in the mutable sand.

Tombolo pushed the throttle full ahead and punched a hole in the night. He pulled a quart of Cuban rum out of the safety gear compartment and passed it around. Eighty-proof laughter, diesel vapors and dreams of un-earned riches forced their recent memories to walk the plank and fall forgotten into a sucking, blue grave.

Quaid looked astern, the luminescent wake spread, like the legs of a welcoming lover and he thought of Dimple Sue.

Beanne sat nearby. He knew he ought to be thinking about being rich but didn't know where he ought to start. Maytag found himself thinking about Moonbeam and her "Great Spirit." Tombolo was drunk and kept pushing the throttle to the stops and Naldo; he just wanted to go home.

An hour later they reached the marina.

~ ~ ~

"Okay, look, here's the deal," Quaid said as Tombolo finished tying *Betty's Boongy* to the dock. He reached down the front of his wet suit, glanced around and groped for the Kevlar bag. "We've got to get rid of these stones and we've got to do it quickly."

Shadowed by Maytag, Naldo sat silently on the dock without a shadow of his own and waited for a chance to slip away.

"How are we going to sell stolen emeralds? Put an ad in the paper? Duh? We really ought to think this one through, Quaid," Beanne said.

"We're pro'essionals, we don't need to think, right Quaid?" Tombolo sought approval.

It was quiet.

"Well, maybe we ought to throw them overboard somewhere in the gulf, wait a few months and then pretend to find them." Beanne offered.

"Nah, that's already been done," Quaid said.

"Oh."

"Who's the strangest person we know who might have a way to get a few bucks out of these green ghosts?"

It was quiet again.

Fischbein

Freddy Fischbein, author, stopped writing when he heard the familiar rumble of a diesel engine. He put his pencil aside, pulled his tent flap open and watched as five people climbed off Quaid Butler's boat and onto the dock across from him. They huddled together, gesturing and glancing over their shoulders, uncertain and nervous.

Freddy had lived in Key West for five years and was experienced in the art of self-deception. Still, he could sense something was going down, and like so many times before, somehow knew he would become involved. Thankfully, Freddy was born with survivor's intuition and a fondness for accessories.

AT THE DOCK

Dimple Sue also recognized B*etty's Boongy* as she motored past the *Spooner Wharf* on the way to the Toxic Triangle docks.

She dropped her apron, grabbed some essentials and headed for the Toxic Triangle. She arrived minutes later out of breath with a leather gun belt slung low on her hips. One holster held a dangling six-pack, the other a six-shooter.

Dimple Sue didn't know Bonterra was in the process of being turdified and drew down on Naldo and Maytag without hesitation. Quaid was impressed. Dimple Sue hadn't told him, or anyone else in Key West, she'd been a deputy sheriff in Odessa, Texas to earn money to attend pole-dancing school. She took out bad guys as often as she took out the garbage. I'm safe in Odessa, she thought, I got family, so let's us have a little fun right now.

"What's it going to be boys, drink or die?" Dimple Sue pulled the hammer back on a snub-nosed revolver with her right thumb and popped a beer tab with the left. Quaid was more impressed.

"Whoa, hold on there, Dimple Sue," Quaid said. "Everything's okay, darlin'. Maytag's come over to our side. I even think he has a crush on Moonbeam, right Maytag?"

"Ugga."

If Maytag blushed at the suggestion no one could tell.

"And Naldo, he just wants to vamoose, right Naldo?" Quaid finished and Naldo nodded.

"You got the stones?" she swung her blond mane and eyeballed Quaid.

"Does the Pope poop in the woods?" Bolo chimed in. "Is a frog's asshole water- tight? ... Right, am I right, Quaid?"

Bolo was not good with metaphors. Everybody cracked up.

"Only the Pope knows," Beanne fired back, "you oughta learn some new jokes, Bolo, that's what you oughta do." His oughtism was back.

'What about the Pope's nose?" Bolo asked. Everybody cracked again.

After they stopped yukking it up, Quaid turned to Dimple Sue, "You betcha we got 'em Dimple Sue, and that's the problem. How can we sell these without getting in even more trouble? We need somebody, somebody really off the beaten path, to handle this weirdness. Someone who doesn't even know there is a box to think outside of."

Everyone looked at Tombolo. He held up one finger as if to accent his forthcoming opinion, then tipped over and went face down in the oyster shells. It was his signature move.

"Simple," said Dimple Sue. She stepped over Tombolo, while admiring his style, "the weirdest dude I know is Freddy. He lives over there," she pointed across the water, "under the dock between the *Coco Loco* and the *Sun Hippie*."

Over the last few months, Dimple Sue had purchased several dozen pages of Freddy's novel, *"Another Beautiful Day in Paradise for You, But Not for Me."*

Freddy described it as a "Meaningless story of self-abuse, hereditary confusion and long term acne."

Dimple Sue liked Freddy and Freddy, who admitted to being "frusterbated" while in her presence, liked Dimple Sue as well, she had plenty style.

"Oh shit, why didn't I think of that?" Quaid said, "Freddy, yeah, you're right, Dimple Sue, if anybody can figure what to do with weird, it's Freddy,"

To the west, the sun set like a sunburned Canadian doing a cannon ball into a motel pool.

"Look," Dimple Sue pointed. "That's him over there, peeking out of his tent fly."

"It's called a flap," Quaid corrected.

"Whatever. Oops! He spotted us. There he goes, back in like a hermit crab." Dimple Sue's fun seeking mind jumped onto the problem like a tick on a hairless dog.

Hi, Ho, Pankersley.

"Let's check Freddy out in the morning," she said.

Quaid glanced around in the dusky light. Maytag and Naldo were gone.

FREDDY OR NOT

Freddy Fischbein worked part time as a male, or female, impersonator depending on the crowd, at O I 8 1 Bar on Duval Street. He was a sight to behold and performed under the Nom De Plume, *Squiffy Dubois and the Key West Pinks.*

Freddy lived underneath a wooden dock in the Toxic Triangle, on the east side of Key West Bight, 100 feet across the water from Quaid's dock. Dock people described him as a "slight of art handist."

The rickety wooden wharf, originally designed for shrimpers to unload their cargoes of Pink Gold (shrimp) and sometimes Square Groupers (pot) became, in later years, a waypoint for human flotsam and jetsam. On a sandy ribbon between wet and dry, the Toxic Triangle harbored land bound lunatics, mind-melded Caribbean drifters and determined Euro-vagabonds who walked the planks in search of, "something."

Freddy's living arrangement was unique even by Toxic Triangle standards. His vessel, *Eartha,* consisted of a 6'X6' pop-up pup tent duct taped to an inflated Queen-sized air bed that, in turn, was wrapped with tarps to protect it from sharp barnacles on the pilings below the dock.

Suspended on small lines, like a spider in the center of its web, Freddy remained hidden from casual view. The large sailing vessel, *Coco Loco,* protected one side and an old shrimp boat, the *Sun Hippie,* protected the other.

Life was tough on the sea-going air bed and even tougher when Freddy tried to pen a few pages of his novel during stormy nights. Writing in the full lotus position with a wet ass sometimes affected his storytelling skills, among other things. Thankfully, the skinny fiberglass tent poles flexed as rolling swells compressed the tent against the underside of the dock. Freddy said it was like living inside a whoopee cushion.

"During one Nor'easter," he was fond of telling, "the tent compressed so fast it blew all my shit out the door and later the same day I saw a famous fishing guide wearing a pair of my custom silk panties on his head down to the Chartroom Bar. Geesh."

In addition to fighting for his life during the occasional storm, Freddy, age 36, remained confused about his sexual orientation and rotated from one to another faster than a gerbil in clothes dryer. Unable to achieve a definitive conclusion, Freddy compensated by donning unique, colorful and sometimes unwashed garments and accessories gleaned from the Salvation Army night-drop boxes. Each piece expressed a particular leaf of the sexual bramble bush that was his life. He'd spent a few nights in one of those boxes during the last cold spell and enjoyed plenty of time to shop.

"There are just too many choices when it comes to sex," Freddy told his first county appointed psychiatrist who, described Freddy's condition as, "gender fluid."

Omnisexual, hydrosexual, transsexual, quadrosexual, monosexual, ambisexual, unisexual, bisexual, let's try again sexual. These unique blends of disenchanted DNA were open to interpretation by both locals and visitors alike, but they offered few real solutions and blanketed the island like a wet piñata.

Freddy's sartorial interpretation of his confusion displayed influences of marginal life styles, un-lived dreams, a fondness for genitalia and natural organic fibers in one weird, walking package. With frizzy orange and black hair, an alligator skin groin cup with human teeth attached worn over a pair of blue neon shorts, mismatched fish net stockings, a Chiquita banana head dress, high-heeled flip flops, tinkling trinkets and a Australian bush knife, Freddy cast an appalling figure among the already appalling inhabitants of the Toxic Triangle. Freddy saw life through the wrong end of a telescope and generated uncalled for glances and comments when he was ashore. When a gawker over-gawked, Freddy always turned sharply and said, "Let ye without sin... buy the fucking drinks!"

Those without sin were remarkably few. Still, it was Freddy's motto and helped keep him sober.

In most cases it was easier to make, "happy ripples," under the dock and contemplate his choices in solitude. On nights calm enough to write, Freddy produced up to ten pages of work, his tedious pencil stub writing interrupted only by the occasional drug deal.

Stomp, stomp, stomp. Three stomps on the planks above his head signaled, "Time for bidness." Freddy wore a hard hat for safety and responded with three taps using his own head. Instantly a damp ten-dollar bill dangled through the planks above the tent door. Freddy snatched the legal tender like a Biafran bonefish and tucked it into his monochromatic G-string stenciled, *"Your guess is as good as mine."*

He opened a red Tupperware container and folded some Opa-Locka Blue into a piece of burnable un-waxed bread paper, smashed it flat with his Bible so it would fit through the crack and passed it to the anxious recipient above. When he heard flip-flops in retreat, he went back to work, writing.

Freddy typically awoke early, re-inflated his air bed, checked his crab trap and fed Fuzzbutt, his de-clawed Siamese cat. After a cup of barnacle and peyote tea, he selected an expressive wardrobe and strutted into town, ready to compete with other early birds for the worm of success. Once in town he stopped to pick up four double *café con leches* at the *Free Frog* coffee bar and shared them with a friend who worked at the nearby Peer House motel. His friend had access to a copy machine.

By nine, with a full-blown caffeine buzz, Freddy walked the streets flogging fresh pages of his novel, *"Another Beautiful Day in Paradise for You, But Not for Me,"* a still warm selection of words written the night before. He usually made enough money for a breakfast of grits and grunts at the *Harry Harpoon* restaurant on Caroline Street.

On this day, Freddy sold 14 pages. Enough to buy breakfast, a yellow note pad with lines, (Freddy loved the lines) and two used pencils with little pink erasers still intact that he employed as stunt double nipples in one of his performance outfits. Freddy also found a pair of fly fisherman's waders at Lucky Bill's Pawnshop. He was tired of writing with a wet ass. Maybe that's what inspired Ernest to get off the beach and into a boat, he thought.

After breakfast, Freddy spent most of the day riffling through Salvation Army drop boxes in search of a tawdry late night ensemble. He had a custom implement, carried down his pant leg that looked like a small flexible harpoon. The tool could reach through the drop box slot and recover chosen items. Freddy was Captain Ahab, in search of the Great White Tank Top.

He returned to *Eartha* late that afternoon, and just before his nap, Freddy heard a soft shuffling on the dock above his head, then suddenly a series of thumps, like a one-legged tap dancer.

Topside, Dimple Sue hopped on one leg and tried to free her other high heeled shoe from a space between the planks without getting slivers in her bare foot. Quaid looked away and pretended to check the weather. They'd been sitting on *Betty's Boongy* watching and waiting for Freddy since ten that morning.

Dimple Sue freed her sling back and spoke toward her painted toes, "Yo, Freddy, you down there? It's Dimple Sue."

"Dimple Sue, wha-zup, girl?"

"I, ah, we need to talk to you."

"We who, and who what?"

"Me, and Quaid Butler."

Several local dock rats, who earned beer money by regularly appearing in line-ups for the city cops, walked past Quaid and Dimple Sue.

"Zup?" One of the usual suspects asked.

"Nada." Dimple Sue smiled.

"We live in Coolness Bay, man," one remarked and moved on.

Dimple Sue waited until they were out of earshot; she knew one of them worked for the DEA.

"It's nothing, really," she said quietly towards her painted toes.

"Well, my goodness, *that* sounds interesting, dear," Freddy replied gaily and reached for his damp needlepoint frame. He had morphed into his grandmother persona. "Come on down, sweetie."

For safety purposes, Granny Freddy watched Dimple Sue climb backwards down the ladder. Her stiletto heels and cut off blue jeans made the task difficult, dangerous and well worth watching.

"Careful dear, take your time and don't punch a nasty hole in my house with those gorgeous shoes!"

The clawless Fuzzbutt scrambled around the air bed trying to keep it balanced while Freddy envisioned the Titanic and all those well-dressed people who lost their wardrobes. What about those wardrobes, where are they now, anyway?

Quaid lay on his stomach, peered over the dock and rolled his eyes like, "What's up?" Freddy smiled out the side of his mouth but never took his eyes off Dimple Sue's descending derriere. "Safety first," he mumbled and monitored her stimulating descent.

"Go slowly and be safey, safey," Freddy encouraged from below.

Even the pulsing water and eternal tides paused to envy Dimple Sue's supple motion.

Dimple Sue played the game, Freddy did not blink or sink, and Quaid waited his turn at the top of the ladder, thankful he'd worn long pants.

Once Dimple Sue settled into a floating lotus position, Quaid descended the ladder and squatted next to her.

"Don't make any sudden movements or we may go down." Freddy said. He put his needlepoint down as Fuzzbutt shifted to the high side.

"So dearie, what's so secret that we have to do it under the dock?" Freddy asked.

"Well," Dimple Sue began, "we have a little problem and it's causing us some worry."

"What kind of worry?"

"The kind of worry that can get us killed," Quaid added.

"That *is* a problem."

Quaid went on, "See, we got these emeralds from an inflatable doll belonging to a Cuban gangster that the sharks ate and we're not sure what to do with them."

"The sharks ate the Cuban, or the doll?"

"The Cuban."

"Damn, food must be scarce, global warming." Freddy said.

Freddy changed his position slowly so as not to disturb *Eartha's* balance or Fuzzbutt's instinct for survival and filled an aluminum pot with water. He placed it on a portable Bunsen burner then twisted into a semi-squat, quasi-lotus pose next to Dimple Sue and watched water boil.

Quaid and Dimple Sue looked at each other but remained silent.

Freddy rummaged through a small jewelry box until he heard boiling, then stopped and put the box in his lap, "You got the stones with you?"

"You betcha, Fred Rider" Quaid grinned.

"Lemme see em," Freddy smiled.

Quaid glanced at Dimple Sue and then at Freddy. "Do you actually know anything about emeralds, Freddy?"

"Course I do."

Satisfied, Quaid opened the bag.

Freddy reached in and took half a dozen stones into his hand.

"Nice." Freddy said and adjusted his position. As he turned, he pocketed the stones and slyly dropped a pair of his favorite chandelier, emerald green, rhinestone earrings and some brown powder into the boiling water.

"Let's have us a little emerald tea, get a beryllium buzz, just you and me," Freddy said in a sing-song voice, "It's what the ancient's did, kid."

Quaid gasped. Dimple Sue instinctively reached for the stones but Quaid stopped her while Freddy stirred the brew with a green eyebrow pencil.

"These stones," he said, "are a green colored form of beryl from which beryllium can be extracted. Emeralds were ground up by well-to-do ancients and put in food or used to make emerald tea, like we're doing 'cept I don't have an emerald grinder so the tea may be a little weak. Anyway, my dad said it cures a few of the many mental afflictions from which the wealthy suffer. He told me emeralds represent spring and rebirth, help men survive at sea and serve as an antidote for latent menopause. But," Freddy eyeballed Quaid, "they also relate with jealousy and can be used to call on the dark forces. On the other hand, American Indians say they are the souls of fireflies in the moonlight."

"How do you know all this shit, Freddy?" Quaid asked.

"My uncle, Irv the Eye, they call him, is a stone dealer on 47th Street in New York, down in the Diamond District."

"Oh, you say your Uncle Irv knows, huh?"

"Yup."

Time stretched like an old Slinky. Freddy stirred slowly. A sweet plume of something caused Freddy's eyes to glow greener with each revolution of the eyebrow pencil and strange lime colored smog filled the tent. Soon Quaid, Freddy and Dimple Sue united in strange and perfect silent harmony below the rotting planks of Old Key West, while waves clapped enthusiastically and barnacles waved a friendly hello.

"We're in a bong," Dimple Sue said.

THE ITCH

The airbed slowly lifted as an itchy manatee bobbed up to scratch itself on the bottom of the bed. The supple tent poles flexed and an explanation, although unnecessary, was simple in physical terms, but to Quaid and Dimple Sue it was a sign.

"I'm really high, I'm gonna unfurl my sails ..." said Dimple Sue.

"Yeah, me too, Simple Dew."

Quaid stared at Dimple Sue and she back at him. Neither recognized the other, but smiled and laughed together without hesitation or restraint.

The itch-free manatee ceased his scrabbling, vented into the dank dock air and settled onto the mud below as Freddy, slyly and unseen, added another pinch or two of peyote powder to the already heady brew. He stirred a while longer, until the fluorescent green eyebrow pencil was almost gone, then poured the infusion into tiny glass Gerber baby food jars and proposed a toast, "To a simple solution, for a difficult problem."

The tea was hot and so were the Gerber's. They each took a quick sip.

"Aiyee!" they cried in painful harmony then stopped and stared at each other. Three green-glowing tongues flashed in the damp half-light like small navigation buoys.

"Green means go!" said Dimple Sue.

"Hoo boy!" Quaid said.

"Ride' em cowboy!" said Freddy.

With lunacy looming and immortality in his belly, Quaid sought comfort in an old Tudor dirge, "He who laughs last, laughs best."

Suddenly, he was afraid to stop laughing.

FORT MEADE, MARYLAND

Commander Lancaster Sudds, a military man to the 'nth degree, stood the last moments of his dog watch between 1800 and 2000 hours EDT. In twenty minutes, or 1200 ticks, he would exit the secure underground structure that was disguised as a putting green for senior officers, nod at the sleeping guard and undergo a friendly, butt thorough, pat down by security officer, Shalandra "Lips" Covet.

On a regular day, after Ms. Covet's insistent prodding, Sudds left work via a hinged urinal in the men's room and climbed a dank set of stairs to a camouflaged exit behind a row of Porta Potty's near hole # 2 adjacent to the sand trap. Sudds always emerged waving an old golf club and although the entire charade was inconvenient, it allowed him to wear golf clothes to work.

"Playing thru!" he always called loudly to quell suspicion.

Once in the parking lot, he deflated his official persona, fired up his 1980 Beemer and returned to his suburban home in Severna Park where both his wife and dog awaited his return. Ironically, both were named Dolly.

He'd owned Dolly the dog, a poodle/beagle mix, for almost two years before he met his wife, Dolly. Although awkward, she'd learned to live with the occasional misunderstanding and waited patiently near her food bowl for Lancaster's return each night. So did the dog.

For Lancaster Sudds, this would not be one of those regular days.

~ ~ ~

"Nork, nork, nork, nork, nork, nork, nork ..." This irksome tone unexpectedly emanated from the giant Q90.3 Maelstrom Vortex main frame computer in Commander Sudds area of responsibility and, deep underground in a small grey air-conditioned room young Army private, Billy "Scooter" Parts, Keeper of the Q, heard the alarm.

He quickly folded his knees to his chest, pushed away from his desk with both feet and coasted across the grey concrete floor.

The six dimensional Q-Aural Observer program monitored incoming satellite data from the government's most secret command known as, (SATDATRATFLATPATIT4TAT,) a surveillance satellite and rocket catering system. Their motto: *TRADIMUS* (We Deliver) has been confirmed and re-affirmed by our enemies, many of whom, it is said, died with the word, SATDATRATFLATPATIT4TAT, on their parched, dung specked lips.

An entourage of twenty technicians, like white-smocked maggots tending to a fat grub queen, monitored the Q 24/7 and the Q, in turn, monitored over 1000 prescribed targets across the Caribbean, Gulf of Mexico, Central America and downtown Key West.

"One Humorous Family" was Key West's official slogan and fallback position. A torpid little island, known to host a clam-bake of unused analytical minds, it is located on the western edge of the mysterious Bermuda Thong Triangle. A petri dish of sub-tropical humanity, Key West, known as *The Isle of Bones,* has always been of interest to those who are interested.

Just in time, Parts spun his 5-roller desk chair and skidded to a stop in front of Commander Sudds. He stood smartly and snapped to attention. It was Private Parts job to keep the quirky Q90.3 running at all costs.

"Sir," Parts piped.

"What is it, Private Parts?" Sudds quietly admired Parts' high speed/low drag maneuver and stifled a grin of approval.

"Sir, it's that *norking* sound ... sir."

"Oh yes, that sound, *norkish* indeed, awoke me rather abruptly I must admit. I was wondering about it myself on the way toward consciousness."

"I haven't heard it before, sir, but we know the *God's Eye* satellite is currently over the Key West area."

"Key West, hum ... not surprising. What do you think it is, private?"

"I don't know, sir."

"What do you mean you 'don't know,' it's your job to know."

"Know what, sir?"

"Look, Parts, this is no time for tomfoolery. Don't we have a freakin' manual? Damn it, Parts, put a chaser on this analmometry, locate the source, advise MASINT (Measure and Signature Intelligence) then repeat the previous pass-over and call me on the second rotation. Set the sky-eye to hi-def-slash- hi-res. Tuck and roll, Parts, tuck and roll."

"Roger that, sir."

"And Parts."

"Sir?"

"Hush-hush and riki-tick!"

"Roger that, sir."

With no concrete idea what Sudds meant, Parts patriotically remounted his chair, pushed off and scooted toward the Q90.3.mv control console 106 feet across the room. If I was diving to 106 feet, he thought, I'd be narced by now. He bested his own single kick-glide ratio by more than 2 seconds during the crossing, but no one noticed the accomplishment, including Parts.

BACK UNDER
THE DOCK

It was only when their feet got wet that Quaid, Dimple Sue and Freddy noticed something amiss and seconds after Dimple Sue instinctively pulled her shoes off, the center of the air bed collapsed and the pup tent floor filled with water. The flaming burner, the equivalent of the *Titanic's* iceberg, tipped over and burnt a hole in the plastic then extinguished as *Eartha* folded in upon herself. She sank slowly until the remaining burnt, rubber-smelling air, trapped in the top half of the tent, was the only thing keeping them afloat. *Eartha* looked like a giant Portuguese Man O' War.

"The air in the tent is gonna leak out quick," Dimple Sue said.

"I know. It was that dang manatee, it must have poked a hole scratching its own fat ass," Quaid mused.

"That was quick." Freddy muttered as he came up for air and floated chin deep in tropical undergarments, "It's like the Titanic. Now I know how it feels!"

"Huh?" Quaid and Dimple Sue said at the same time.

"Well, we have to dive down and try to get out the door," Quaid said, "or we cut the top open and all squeeze through at the same time."

"Cut it!" Freddy screamed as he tossed Fuzzbutt out and up.

"Okay, Quaid, I'm with you," Dimple Sue said with revirginated enthusiasm. She looked forward to a little

113

"squeezing" with Quaid, even if it was life or death. But then again, she thought, what isn't "life or death" and got ready to go.

"Okay, I'll make the cut and ..." Quaid paused to check on Dimple Sue. She held her red sling-backs above her head. Her blonde hair floated around her upturned breasts like wheat fields around a barn.

"They're Jimmy Choo's, for Christ's sake," she glared at Quaid and Freddy "And they ARE NOT waterproof, OK?" she said defiantly.

"Whose shoes?" asked Freddy.

"Jimmy Choo's shoes!"

"Whose?"

"Cut it out you guys, we're about to drown." Quaid said.

Before Quaid could find his knife, the manatee that had molested them earlier returned. Perhaps it was the same one, who scorned by Maytag, returned for vengeance and another ungracious hump. Hell hath no fury like a manatee scorned.

Through the tent bottom, Dimple Sue could feel the rough, barnacled back with her bare feet; she *hoped* it was his back.

Slowly, whether by intent, accident or the need to scratch, no one will ever know, the manatee silently rose from the depths to save them.

"Going up! Cosmetics, shoes, ladies lingerie..." Freddy quipped vivaciously as the aforementioned items floated past his face. Freddy, though, was a tough and unforgiving little fuck and suddenly kicked wildly at the buoyant mammal.

"I hope you choke on my panties!" He screamed at the manatee.

Freddy Fischbein's cries drew dockside residents who began to gather on the planks overhead, like buzzards in flip flops.

Luckily, the three were able to overcome their earring and peyote buzz and stand upright on the manatees back. Pressed together like clothed sardines they struggled out the tent flap and up the ladder.

Fuzzbutt, waited patiently above, dry as a bone. The cat stood facing away from the ladder and each soaked survivor was treated to a polite smattering of applause and the classic ! as they emerged onto the splintered boards.

Even though it was getting dark, Freddy grabbed a bait net and ran to salvage the beloved *Eartha* and his seagoing wardrobe.

"I'm going to go to FEMA after I salvage *Eartha* and get another rig, you'll have to sign for me, Quaid, and then I'm going to sue the shit out of that damn manatee. I hate rodents! No respect!" Freddy yelled over his shoulder.

~ ~ ~

The last few minutes with Freddy had not gone well and they left him trying to net his bag of peyote and Elton John feather boa.

Quaid and Dimple Sue walked without words to *Betty's Boongy* and changed into dry clothing.

Dimple Sue looked real good in Quaid's oversize cargo shorts and T-shirt with the words *"Definition of Confidence: The feeling you have before you understand what is going on."*

They ambled to the *Spooner* and took a table near the water. Quaid felt strangely at ease, peaceful almost. Everything was totally screwed up and this he was used to. It was his bailiwick, his wheelhouse, his ...

"You got the emeralds, Quaid?" Dimple Sue whispered.

Quaid looked down and frowned, "What do you think?" he said meekly.

"Oh no! Oh, hell no! Say it ain't so, Quaid!"

Quaid looked up and grinned. He liked it when Dimple Sue got riled up and her cheeks got red.

"Yeah, I got 'em, Miss Dimple Sue, except for the ones Freddy took. That was some tea, huh?"

It was quiet. After a moment, Dimple Sue went vertical and tweaked toward the bar.

Well, at least the next dive won't be to 206, Quaid thought. He knew he would have to help Freddy in the morning, and although he'd never salvaged an air bed before, he was confident he could overcome any problem. What can go wrong in eight feet of water?

Dimple Sue returned with four drinks. They hammered down two Deep Air daiquiris each without toasting or even looking up. After a few moments, Dimple Sue shook her wet hair, stood and headed for the ladies room. Quaid started thinking, but before he could really get going, Dimple Sue returned. Quaid hid a grin.

"There are no dang paper towels, only that old hand dryer," she explained. Her long, wild corn-silk blond hair looked as if she'd been under a helicopter when it took off.

She complained of a kink in her neck and sat down with a pout. Her shorts were wet from sitting on the floor under the dryer.

"Quaid?"

"What?"

"Can I ask you a question?"

"It would be better if you didn't."

"No, seriously, listen ... things aren't so bad, are they?"

"No, things aren't **so** bad, they're **real** bad."

"We're not dead and we did get a helluva buzz."

"That's encouraging, but you forgot the yet part."

They talked like this until the adrenaline faded and the fog of booze rolled in. With no good ideas and a massive hangover on the horizon they finished their drinks and Quaid walked Dimple Sue home.

"That was an exciting date. You want to come in, Quaid?"

"You know I do, Miss Dimple Sue, but maybe I should just put on my thinking cap instead."

"Is that what you call a condom, a thinking cap?"

Quaid paused and garfooned deeply. The remark was truer than he'd ever imagined. That's why he loved women; they were always reading your mind, even if you didn't have one.

"You're funny, but ..."

"You think my butt's funny?" Dimple Sue asked with a grin.

"I, ah, no, I mean are you sure?"

"You ain't scared of little ol' Dimple Sue, are you?"

"Guess we'll find out, won't we? Being scared is normal, it's what I do." Quaid smiled and nodded towards the cottage.

"OK, baby cakes and Quaid ... what does 'Blow and Go mean, anyway?" Dimple Sue, batted her salty lashes and gave him a quick peck on the lips.

The screen door creaked closed and did not creak again until an hour before dawn.

~ ~ ~

An early morning fisherman's wake rolled Quaid out of his bunk on *Betty's Boongy*. He'd returned to the boat earlier and grabbed a quick nap before the sun came up.

Quaid awoke slowly. Yesterday's passionate night had morphed into today's shit storm. It was time to resolve the mess he was in. Quaid stretched like a soft shell turtle and looked around. Tombolo slept peacefully in the forward V berth. I'll let him sleep, Quaid thought and pulled a long blond hair out of his teeth. First I have to help Freddy he thought and got ready for Freddy just as the VHF radio crackled to life. It was a back-country guide Quaid knew who angled for bonefish on the flats.

"US Coast Guard, this is the fishing vessel *Bad to the Bone*, come in, over."

"*Bad to the Bone, Bad to the Bone* this is the United States Coast Guard Sector Key West, over."

"Coast Guard this is *Bad to the Bone*. I'd like to report a manatee wearing a pup tent swimming between Tank Island and Christmas Tree Island, over."

"You say you found a manatee wearing a pup tent? Is that correct, sir, over?"

"Yup, over."

"Sir, have you been drinking, over, or over drinking, over?"

"Nope, but now that you mention it ..." Quaid could hear a pop-top pop in the background.

He turned away from the radio and dropped his shorts, hid them along with the stones inside the bait well, then slipped into his wetsuit, grabbed his dive gear and knife. He borrowed a neighbor's small outboard boat and headed across the harbor. He knew the animal would drown or starve if it were entangled in the air bed for much longer.

It took only eight minutes to reach the manatee and already locals had gathered and were trading recipes. Some started cooking fires.

Quaid anchored near the manatee and jumped into the water. Within a few moments the manatee was freed from the tangled mess and although the animal seemed thankful Quaid remembered Maytag's encounter and did not turn his back on the creature.

There wasn't much left of Freddy's world. The mass settled slowly to the bottom as a few stray undergarments including a 1989 Fantasy Fest G-String floated to the surface. The sodden items were immediately scooped up and donned by a nearly naked Frenchman known as, *Arrghnow*, the Pirate King of Christmas Tree Island.

Once he put the small boat away, Quaid contacted Bolo, Beanne and Dimple Sue. They agreed to meet at the *Spooner Wharf* later in the day, after Dimple Sue got off work.

Quaid went to find Freddy. He asked around but no one had seen him since the night before.

No one ever saw Freddy again.

~ ~ ~

A black rotary telephone rang in a dingy office on 47th Street in New York City.

"*Shalom.*"

"Uncle Irv, is that you?"

"Freddy!"

THE HUNT

A trio of toughened gangsters departed South Miami at 6 A.M. They'd made their bones on the hard, hot streets of Miami and were often summoned to handle the *negocio sucio,* the dirty business, work that must be done in order to maintain the unpleasant reputation that gangsters and attorneys enjoy so much.

Miguel, Pepe and Chi-Chi traveled in a plain white van that would easily blend with hundreds of other plain white vans and their multi-colored occupants on the way to repair thousands of plain white appliances in multi-colored neighborhoods.

These men, soldiers in the violent *Taco Blanco* cartel, were bound for Key West to locate Iggy Bonterra, Naldo and some clown called Maytag. The bosses in Miami had briefed Miguel. They weren't sure who had the stones but if Miguel could locate Bonterra it would be a start and help get the Columbians off *Taco Blanco's back.*

Miguel Nomorales drove the van. Pepe Garrido rode shotgun while Chi-Chi Chorizo sat in the back on a pile of mulch bags. Both Pepe and Chi-Chi sported the classic, Third World Thug garb, while their leader, Miguel, modeled a traditional khaki British gentleman's jungle outfit, a walking stick modified to accommodate his lack of vertical achievement and an oversized pith helmet.

Miguel spoke perfect Queen's English, absorbed after listening to thousands of BBC commentators during his childhood days in a small third world country known as Carnooba.

At age eighteen, he immigrated to the states where he would be free to become a criminal with a respected accent. Standing five-foot-six with a Castro beard, stiff-upper-lip British enunciation, no eyebrows and white rhinestone sunglasses, Miguel's first impression was sometimes disconcerting.

He turned quickly towards Pepe and Chi-Chi. His pith helmet remained facing forward.

"I say old beans," Miguel began, tapping the dash with his walking stick, "or *frijoles,* if you wish, ha, ha, good fun what? We are about to pop into Key West proper. Does anyone have any questions regarding our mission?"

"Sí," said Chi-Chi, who chomped cheap gum non-stop and squatted on a mulch bag in the back, "I do. What eez eet?"

"Well now, that's a bit of a sticky wicket, isn't it, Chi-Chi? Don't you remember what we discussed and when we discussed it?"

"Sí, I am disgusted too."

"Chi-Chi, old sod, you need to learn proper English, you know. Anyway, we're going to find out where Bonterra and the other chaps have gone and what happened to the stones. We know he was staying at an inn called the Gripps Hotel and that is where we shall begin our quest, our journey of fulfillment, any more questions?"

"Sí," Chi-Chi said, "do we get to kill some peeples?"

"Peeples? Yes, peeples indeed! Well, first we must find these, these *peeples,* don't you agree old chap?"

"Si?"

The entrance to Key West looked like the back lot of a cheap carnival as the van wheeled its way onto the southernmost hemorrhoid. Frayed and flapping banners advertised everything from sex change kits to dental implants. The tattered and forgotten hangings dangled from broken fences while litter and debris, stirred by the constant traffic, dusted statue-like construction workers forever leaning on their shovels.

Miguel located the Gripps Hotel and pulled into the lush tropical parking lot. Chickens, cats, dogs and homeless "Shruburbians" scattered into the weeds.

From the passenger seat, Pepe spotted a free-range chicken and reached for his gun.

Miguel caught the movement. "Pepe, not now, for God's sake, man!"

"I hungry."

"Not now old chap, simply isn't done, poor form, that sort of thing."

Leaving Pepe and Chi-Chi to mind the van, Miguel climbed out, adjusted his pith helmet and set his upper lip on maximum stiffness. He approached the shabby registration desk and tapped the rusted bell. Ding.

A string-bean skinny, cigar chewing front desk clerk slipped through a beaded door wearing a yellowed Frog's Breath t-shirt and a green Speedo. He stood a foot taller than Miguel and had a voice like a dentist's drill.

"Kin I hep ya?"

"I say old chap, looking for a friend of mine, you may have seen him."

"May have, or may not have, depends on for whom the bell tolls." Stringbean coughed.

"Hemingway fan I see. Indeed. Don't mean to be rude, old bean, but I highly recommend you assist me in this endeavor thus avoiding having your nuts cooked over a camp fire while you're still wearing them."

"Well, ain't you the fussy one. Who is it you want?"

"His name is Bonterra. He was with a couple of other chaps."

The clerk thumbed through a stack of hand written, roach chewed, yellow registrations.

"Well, lookee here." Stringbean held up a sheet of paper, "This fella Bonterra's been around for almost one week. Fella paid cash money right up front. "

"What room is he in?"

"He's got the Scent House Suite, but I haven't seen him or his buddies lately."

"I'm sure you meant to say, the Penthouse Suite, old chap."

"Yup, nope, it's the Scent House Suite, nice view, big and private, but she sits two blocks downwind from old Jim Hale's pigeon barn.

"I see. Would you mind terribly if I were to check his room?"

"What are you, some kinda preevert?"

"Remember the camp fire story?"

"Here's the key, go fuck yourself."

Miguel hesitated and then smashed the lobby bell with his walking stick. Ding.

He paused, inhaled deeply, unclenched his fists, crossed the lobby and headed up the stairs. Bonterra's door was unlocked. Miguel opened the door and met the Stink.

"Good god, man! That indeed, is a fowl odor. How could anyone live amongst such inconsiderate stench?"

A cursory glance showed nothing unusual except for a bloody paper picnic table cover, some cigar butts and a crushed sofa. It was breezy in the Scent House where cheap cigar odor mixed with the already overpowering stench of bird. The smell made it difficult for Miguel to concentrate. Pay attention double O, he told himself and methodically examined the room and furniture, including the drawers and closets. Again, nothing unusual, just typical toiletries, dirty laundry, cheap cigar butts and four .38 caliber bullets that nestled against the base of the toilet bowl.

Bonterra had been fooling with the gun while taking a dump. He'd dropped the bullets and forgot to put them all back in the gun he'd given Naldo.

About to leave the room, Miguel noticed a folded matchbook under one leg of a table near the kitchen. He bent down and unfolded it.

THE FLY STRIP LOUNGE, HANG OUT, CATCH A BUZZ! YOU'LL WANT TO STICK AROUND.

It wasn't much, but it was something. Miguel returned to the front desk and slapped at the remnants of the bell.

Stringbean appeared through a beaded curtain.

"Yeah?"

"I say old chap, have you heard of an establishment called the *Fly Strip Lounge*?"

"Oh yeah, it's just down on the waterfront at Gorton's." he pointed, "Some call it the *Losers Lobby*."

"Thank you veddy much old chap, you've been most helpful, and oh, incidentally, keep your mouth shut."

Stringbean studied Miguel's expression, decided a clever rejoinder was not in order and pointed again towards the water.

Miguel walked back to the van. He heard salsa music booming from inside and noticed Chi-Chi had written the words EET ME with chewed gum wads on the inside of the back window. He also saw his own reflection and the embarrassing, wet rings around the armpits of his new, breathable and supposedly vented, jungle outfit. Miguel shook his head and opened the door. It smelled like hot Juicy Fruit gum and hot wet mulch which was only slightly more palatable than the recent aroma of bird shit and cigars.

~ ~ ~

Being the leader, Miguel turned on the AC, put the van in gear and headed towards the waterfront. There's no point in briefing these two idiots, he thought, since they have the same attention span as a housefly.

FLY STRIP

It didn't take long to locate the *Fly Strip* or for Miguel to ingratiate himself with the locals. His doddering old Englishman persona was quite charming and most people felt comfortable around him and were inclined to help the odd looking foreigner who had appeared, like a friendly fungus, amongst them.

Fire Ant sat at the end of the *Fly Strip* bar. It was a calm summer day, very little bobbing going on. Still living high on his recent windfall, he'd had a few beers and did not notice his sweaty elbows begin to slide apart as he listened to some blithering Englishman work his way around the establishment, stopping to speak loudly with almost everyone. Finally, the babbler drew close and Fire Ant overheard his conversation.

"I say old beans." the stranger said to a group of local ladies wearing only Notre Dame tank tops, flowered hats and Hawaiian thongs, "Simply popped in on vacation, don't you know, lovely spot, Key West, anyway, I'm looking for a chap I met years ago, out East, Burma I believe it was, old China hand you might say, has anyone perchance spotted a fat bloke named Bonterra or a skinny bloke called Naldo?" He tapped the table with his cane to hold the ladies attention as bluebottle flies dive bombed their conch salads and no see um's chewed their tender white ankles.

"I saw I think I saw some skinny looking dude down on the docks," one lady said and a smashed a bluebottle with her elbow.

Fire Ant didn't know the whole story, but he'd heard enough scuttlebutt around the docks to know this could be bad news for Quaid Butler and his crew. He was worried and decided to inform Quaid, but before he could slip away, his elbows lost traction and he hit the bar with his jaw. It knocked him out.

Between the beers, the buzz and the bump, Fire Ant did not awaken for some time and when he did temporarily forgot what he had intended to do. By then the cane-tapping Brit was gone.

Chi-Chi and Pepe walked the waterfront, avoided broken planks and listened for comments from boaters and the numerous Cuban fishermen who made this area their base.

Both Chi-Chi and Pepe understood the rapid fire Spanish conversation Cubans are noted for, and incidentally, both spoke English quite well, but didn't, because they were tired of listening to Miguel's offending accent as he droned on and on. If they talked, he talked, more.

The pair knew what they had to do, and would do it. Bang- bang, bye-bye.

As they reached the end of the collapsing boardwalk, Chi-Chi heard a distinct tapping and turned to find Miguel hurrying towards them.

"I say chappies," Miguel said with a bright smile on a dark face, "I do believe we have a breakthrough, a chance, a roughhewn clue that only one of my limber demeanor and inherent charisma could extract from an unknown bevy of bouncy white bosoms. Men, we are now looking for ... *Betty's Boongy!*"

"Sí," Pepe said, "I always looking for dee boongy too."

"Indeed, indeed my good fellow, but this is a particular *Boongy*. It's a vessel called, *Betty's Boongy* and she is painted red."

They covertly scanned the harbor, and there, just beyond the ferro-cement schooner, *Coco Loco* and the old shrimp boat, *Sun Hippie*, was a red hulled motor boat, tied alongside another rotted wooden dock.

TURDIFIED

Unlike some movie heroes, Quaid could not smell danger. He thought it probably smelled like dog shit, or his first ex-wife's perfume. But he could hear it. Danger was a silent tone, a noiseless arrow only the prey perceived and usually an instant too late.

Quaid heard that silent note as three men, who clearly did not belong among the waterfront horde, approached *Betty's Boongy*. He reached for his spear gun, slid it behind his back, then tapped his bare foot on the deck in Morse code, SOS- *dot dot dot-dash dash dash-dot dot dot*, hoping to signal the sleeping Tombolo below. He got a sliver in his big toe trying to make a dash.

As the triad neared the boat, Quaid bent to pry a squished cockroach off his insole and saw no one carried anything threatening in their hands. The smallest of the trio stepped forward and nodded politely. Quaid nodded in return. Not wanting to be left out, Pepe and Chi-Chi also nodded. When the five realized they looked like idiots they stopped abruptly and cleared their throats.

Unfortunately, during his final nod, Miguel's pith helmet fell off, bounced hard against *Boongy's* hull and plopped in the oily water alongside. Pepe and Chi-Chi were momentarily blinded by the sun's reflection off Miguel's hereditary bald spot.

Quaid kept his eye on the strangers and waited for them to make the first move. He hoped Tombolo would remain hidden, recognize the international distress signal and spring into action if necessary.

The sound of the helmet bouncing on the hull disturbed Tombolo more than the Quaid's ineffective, flat-footed tapping had. He awoke abruptly, flatulated in a grotesque manner, mounted his flip flops and leapt out the cabin door. Tombolo was a warrior at heart.

While the others stood in silent disbelief, Tombolo, followed by his recent gastrointestinal absurdity, grabbed the boat hook, assessed the situation, spied the bobbing pith helmet and hurled the boat hook like a harpoon. He missed and hit the beer cooler on the aft deck.

"Those hats are made outta cork, ya know," Tombolo went for the boat hook. "Should 'loat till I can get a harpoon in her," he said and pursed his lips. "Remember Moby Dick? Call me Fishmeal!" he said with pride at his pronunciation.

Tombolo had been out late and was not yet recovered from being over-served. Quaid abruptly checked the weather when Bolo bent to recover the boat hook.

A gentle tropical breeze blew the *"Eau de Bolo"* tang across *Betty's Boongy* and onto the dock. Chi-Chi and Pepe coughed dramatically and held their noses. Exposed barnacles abandoned their shells and swam for deeper water, sea gulls screeched and swerved away.

"Bit of a nasty gust! Tropic breeze indeed! Good Heavens, Man!" Miguel fanned his face, "That type of thing is simply not done, poor form. What? Simply uncalled for," he said and pulled out a hankie, wrapped around a gun.

Bent over the gunwale, bare-ass naked with flip flops in the air and a boathook in his hands, Tombolo appeared to be in an awkward and indefensible position, but somehow he saw the gun. Before the little fella above could say anything further, Tombolo leaned forward and drove the boat hook upwards through a crack between the rotted planks. The rusted, galvanized steel hook stopped one inch beyond the design apex of Miguel's jungle trousers inseam.

He got taller and looked like a khaki corndog on a stick. His gun flipped into the water. *Ploink.*

Pepe and Chi-Chi shifted uncomfortably, Miguel couldn't shift at all and gave a series of high pitched, undecipherable instructions. Tombolo kept the pressure on as Quaid produced the spear gun from behind his back and pointed the barbed tips at the other two. It was an old triple band, double shaft, *Arbalete Champion* with carbon steel spears, sometimes used to hunt elephants or water buffalo in the bush. Chi-Chi and Pepe stared at the glinting spear tips like chickens down a line in the dirt. Neither had ever considered being speared.

"Okay now, you two," Quaid waved the spear gun at Pepe and Chi-Chi, "stand one in front of the other and spoon, you savvy? You know why you boys are standing in line? It's because I can shoot you both at once. Save spears and reduce my carbon steel footprint," Quaid said. "Now do it, snuggle! Make up your minds, quick," Quaid snapped. "This trigger gets kinda tricky after being in salt water so much."

A pushing match ensued regarding who would be in front, but they finally spooned as ordered. Pepe was in front.

No one noticed a film crew setting up cameras nearby.

~ ~ ~

Quaid paused, flexed his index finger and looked at the three suspicious characters. He hated to be judgmental, they could be Bible salesman for all he knew, but the Brit's gun and the bulges under his cronies' untucked shirts may have influenced his profiling.

"So, the way things are set up right now is, if we can't figure this out peacefully, all three of you clowns will be turdified by dawn." Quaid nodded at the always hungry barracudas patrolling the bulkhead.

Pepe turned to look over his shoulder. Chi-Chi shrugged. *Madre de la Frijole!*

"Turdified?" Chi-Chi repeated quietly.

"I know you boys come in peace, so let's put all those *pieces* in the water. Drop 'em, right now!"

Plop, plop, plop. Two guns and a wad of Juicy Fruit gum hit the water at the same time.

Quaid didn't say much, but when he did, most living people figured it was better to just listen.

"Now, stick your hands in each other's front pants pockets and stand real still. "You move, I shoot, comfucking-prendo?" Quaid knew if these losers tried to pull a knife they would probably cut each other's nuts off in the process.

"*Sí,*" the pair said. These were the first words spoken.

Ah, hah, Latinos! Quaid thought.

It didn't take long to put two and two together. Unfortunately, he came up with three.

"Turdified, not sure I know the term, old bean," Miguel interrupted with a thin voice. Quaid squinted like Clint Eastwood. It hurt his eyes but worked.

"OK, ease off, Bolo. Let's talk." He eyeballed Miguel. "And you two." Quaid shifted the spear gun and one-eyed the other two. "Don't move."

Quaid slowly lowered the spear gun while Bolo removed the boat hook from Miguel's prodded parts.

The leader settled gratefully onto his platform jungle boots and sighed. Miguel was cool, always had been, and steadfastly refused to participate in his own demise.

"What do you boys want? I know you're not selling Girl Scout cookies." Quaid asked.

"Funny you should say that. I do feel a bit of gnawing in the belly. Loosening of the bowels, that sort of thing, don't you know? Have you any tea and crumpets handy?"

Miguel asked, maintaining both his dignity and sense of humor.

Bolo finished scooping Miguel's pith helmet out of the brackish water. The helmet normally weighed less than a pound, but when wet weighed five times that. Tombolo handed the damp pith to Miguel who nodded and quickly put it on his sun-sensitive head.

"Good heavens, bit of a gaff, what!" an embarrassed Miguel exclaimed, as oily harbor water with several small jellyfish poured over his head and landed on his feet.

Pepe and Chi-Chi snickered in the background while Miguel drip dried. After a few moments Miguel went on, "Actually, old bean, we've come to recover some property and we think you may know where it is."

Tombolo hopped onto the dock, climbed on top of a dumpster and like Moby Dick's harpooner *Queequeg* in the bow of a whale boat, stood poised and ready for action. Tombolo did not suffer from projectile dysfunction.

"What kind of property?" Tombolo asked.

Instead of tattoos like *Queequeg's, Tombolo's* sun darkened torso was covered with pale white scars, but his back was baby-butt smooth. Tombolo never turned from a fight, but Quaid thought, he should have put his shorts on.

The definition of confidence popped into Quaid's mind and reminded him he had some thinking yet to do. Therefore, instead of making a snap decision, he offered a truce.

"Truce, anyone?"

"*Sí, sí, sí!*"

As the two thugs disentangled, the unintentionally offended Pepe slapped at Chi-Chi, while Miguel practiced how to walk with five pounds on his head. Finally, Tombolo put the boat hook down, "Let's do some bidness," he said, grabbed his shorts off the safety rail and motioned the trio onboard and into the cabin. Quaid stood aside to allow the guests to go below. He smiled when he noticed three small oil slicks on the water's surface where the guns had been dropped or tossed. The sea will eat anything, he thought. He grabbed his cell phone called Beanne, told him to find Dimple Sue and come to the boat ASAP.

Quaid could hear Tombolo practicing his Cockney accent with Miguel and paused a moment longer to deliberate. Shortly, he turned to go below and found Tombolo being restrained by Chi-Chi, while Pepe held a glinting fillet knife to his throat.

Shit, Quaid thought, that's my good fish knife!

"OK, fish-face, maybe now you want to talk, eh?" Pepe challenged Quaid and waved the knife hypnotically in front of Tombolo's face. Tombolo's eyes crossed.

"Nope, don't think so." Quaid said and nodded at Bolo. Tombolo nodded and took a quiet, deep breath. Quaid stepped back, slammed the heavy teak cabin door shut, flipped the latch and secured it with a marlin spike. There was no escape from below. The front hatch was permanently sealed to keep water out and the port lights were closed tight to keep mosquitoes at bay. Before anyone could say "Huh?" Quaid grabbed a fire extinguisher from the lazarette and fired half a dozen vigorous blasts of CO_2 into the cabin through the starboard ventilator. He hoped he remembered his deep sea training and correctly calculated how long someone can go without oxygen before passing out.

It wasn't long before he heard a metallic clink, that's the knife, Quaid thought, then a thump, then a "Tally Ho, thump!", that's Miguel, then another, then another. After the fourth thump that sounded like an over-cooked quail hitting the kitchen floor, Quaid thought it safe and opened the companionway door.

In less than one minute they'd crumpled like cheap beach balls. All four lay face down on the cabin sole and thankfully, Quaid supposed, there should be no brain damage other than that which existed prior to the deck dive.

Quaid turned on the cabin fan, dragged a lethargic Tombolo on deck and slapped the emergency O2 mask on his face. Bolo nodded, he'd held his breath as long as he could. He was basically okay. Quaid stood on deck and waited for the bad guys to regain consciousness and for Beanne and Dimple Sue to arrive.

Inside the cabin, the trio of oxygen deprived idiots' slowly reclaimed awareness until Quaid, tired of waiting, hosed them down, speeding up the process. "You assholes tired of screwing around yet?"

This was not the beginning of negotiations he had hoped for.

~ ~ ~

0242 hours, Fort Meade, Maryland

Commander Lancaster Sudds' cell phone rang. He knew nothing good ever happened at this time of night.

Sudds rolled away from his comfortable spooning position, completed a full one-eighty rotation and reached for his phone, but missed. The sleeping Dolly's were jarred awake by Lancaster's unimpaired, naked impact on the cold hardwood floor.

Always the soldier's wife, Mrs. Dolly also performed a one-eighty, with full gainer and double scooch and answered the phone.

"The Sudds residence, hold on." She rolled backwards to let little Dolly the dog, out from under her compressed cleavage. "Send your message."

"Ah, Mrs. Sudds, ah, this is P-p-p-Private Parts," the soldier stuttered.

Commander Sudds rolled onto his back.

"Oh! My God!" Dolly's mouth dropped open revealing healthy pink gums, her eyes widened and she screamed, then threw the secure, encrypted, military specification phone against the wall. The well armored phone dented the dry wall, bounced back and hit Lancaster in the groin.

Lancaster cupped his package with both hands and rolled to face the bed, "What's wrong dear? Who was that?" Sudds squeaked and massaged his most recent bruise. Since he couldn't get up, he decided to stay on the floor.

"There was some kind of preevert on the phone, Lanny, he was talking about, oh, oh, oh my god, he was talking about private parts, Lanny, private parts!" She grasped the remnants of her once great chest and looked aghast.

Sudds eyes widened, "Did you say Private Parts?"

Dolly looked down and noticed the location of Lancaster's purely medicinal hands.

"Oh God, oh no, oh shit, not you too, Lanny, this is simply too much even for a patriot." She grabbed her polyester house coat, teeth and vibrator, disguised as a hand grenade and headed for the couch.

Lancaster Sudds clambered off the floor and donned his Arnold Palmer dress uniform. Sudds preferred not to be naked when issuing orders. He carried his spit-shined spiked golf shoes in his hand. It was 0249. Sudds noted his reflection in the bathroom mirror, "I look like a flower without water." he mumbled and scratched his day-old, double chin stubble.

Sudds' set his face in grim determination. It is my duty, he remembered, to respond and garner a SITREP, a situation report. Sudds could not find his glasses but grabbed the phone off the floor and dialed by feel. The phone rang longer than it should.

"Hello, big guy, horny? Wanna fu...?"

"Parts, is that you?"

"What kind of parts are you looking for sweetie?" a soft, wet voice asked.

"Private Parts and don't fuck around, you called me, what's the SITREP?"

"Private parts, my goodness, and SITREPS too! Lordy, lordy, you DO need mama, oh my! Wanna do the nasty on the phone?"

It was then, and only then, Sudds realized the depth of his misunderstanding and although profoundly embarrassed, hit the *save contact* icon, in case he decided to prosecute later, then hung up and took a deep breath. A second dialing produced better results.

"G-g-g-good mo- mo- morning, sir and or mam. This is Private P-P-P-Parts, duty officer. Code 11221 SATDATRATFLATPATIT.4.TAT. This is a non-s- s-secu …"

"Cut the shit, Parts, its Commander Sudds. What's happening?"

"P-p-p-please provide personal input security code for te-te-telephonic verif …"

"For fucks sake, Parts, it's me."

"No offense sir, b-b-but do you know how many m-m-me's are out there?"

Sudds could see his point. He also saw the man was overly excited. Parts always stuttered when he was nervous. Sudds tried to calm him as he headed for the front door.

"Parts?"

"Sir?"

"What do you wish to report?"

The s-signal is c-c-coming from K-K-Key West."

The endless stuttering drove Sudds mad, "Parts, cease verbal communication. Go dark, use M Code, Roger?

"Dark, Sir?"

"Stay on the phone and tap your message in Morse code on the dial pad, got it? And Parts, hush- hush, riki-tick."

Parts turned off the lights; he didn't need them anyway, and tapped away in the electronic darkness. "... — - ..."

Lancaster Sudds pocketed his phone, passed by the couch and patted Dolly on the ass. She turned and snapped at him.

The dog, on the other hand, was already asleep and missed the whole thing. Sudds checked for gum marks and headed for the Beemer.

~ ~ ~

Unfortunately, Chi-Chi and Pepe fell upon each other when they passed out and another scuffle ensued as they came to. On the bright side, neither was recovered enough to do any harm and instead they bickered like pissed-off Chihuahuas. Miguel eyed the fire extinguisher outside the companionway door but decided against using it on the tropical twits since he might need them later.

And this chap Quaid, rather a clever fellow, Miguel thought.

With embarrassed sounds and insincere smiles the dazed trio clambered from the cabin. Chi-Chi and Pepe immediately jumped onto the dock and headed for the bushes to get away from each other and seek relief.

"'Well played old chap, jolly good wicket, what?" Miguel said to Quaid and tugged at his inseam, his, not Quaid's. He stretched like an old snake then recoiled and went below to recover his pith helmet.

"Tally ho!"

Miguel's jungle outfit dried quickly. Pepe and Chi-Chi were not so lucky and stood on the dock in the sun, arms spread like old cormorants drying their wings and were thus posed when Dimple Sue and Beanne arrived. Chi-Chi and Pepe dropped their arms not wanting to look like idiots, too late.

Miguel emerged from the cabin, donned his pith helmet and stepped onto the dock. He remembered to be very careful since he had never learned to swim. I should learn how, just to be safe, he thought and joined Quaid and the others under an old gumbo limbo tree near the bulkhead. Dimple Sue was quiet. Quaid had told her how he'd foiled the bad guys and she was impressed.

"Cool idea," she whispered.

God's tanning lamp was deadly hot, but Tombolo chose to stand in the rays, boat hook at the ready.

"Bolo ought to get in the shade," Beanne said.

"He ought to be in the movies old bean that is where the lad ought to be!" Miguel injected cheerfully.

"Ha, ha, ha." Everyone had a good laugh, except Bolo who launched the boat hook and tried to spear a wharf rat. He was pissed. They were right back where they started, screwed.

"How'd he know my name?" Beanne nodded towards Miguel.

"He meant bean, like the legume, not Beanne like the Billy." Quaid said.

"Oh. What's a legume?"

TALL PAUL

This type of meaningless conversation could've gone on for hours if not for the stealthy, but nonetheless obvious, approach of a recently painted VW van. The van, painted black on one dented side had the letters SMAT, obviously stenciled by a dyslexic artist, on the side.

Quaid and the others turned to see four men, wearing undersized black t-shirts, take turns climbing out the driver's door. The other exits were apparently broken. It took a few moments. The letters **F.I.B.** (the artist again) were ironed on the front of their shirts. It appeared dyslexia ran rampant amongst the leadership.

The men strode toward the group in a familiar *salsa* formation Dimple Sue noted and each carried a black automatic pistol at their side. Quaid froze. He recognized the ordinance; they were the dreadful MKI.1 /CI paintball guns from the early seventies. The red tips were painted black. Quaid choked back laughter and remained frozen in place. Armed men were in front, with only water behind.

"You da boss?" The tallest asked Miguel.

Miguel nodded, "And whom, may I ask, the fuck are you, old chap?"

"I am no one, but I represent the *Malo Muffin Cartel* out of Findley, Ohio, so give me the shit! OK?" the leader demanded in an oddly familiar voice.

Quaid couldn't hold it any longer. He staggered aimlessly, like a happy drunk to distract their attention and wandered near a water hose, coiled on the dock. With action born of desperation, and the funniest thing he'd ever seen, Quaid grabbed the hose and turned to face the four gunmen.

"One move and I'll hose you down," Quaid said in a quiet voice.

"Tall Paul ... is that you?" Dimple Sue asked.

Quaid pointed the hose at him and the man pulled his facemask part way up.

"Paul, what are you doing?" Dimple Sue asked.

It was Paul and he was embarrassed so he fired a symbolic paintball into the air to vent his frusterbation and in memory of his dog, "For Lady Barfly," he said quietly.

Above, in the darkening sky, one of Jim Hale's white racing pigeon unexpectedly found itself with a green ass. The startled bird would surely be taunted by his owner and not allowed to fly at weddings until his ass, like all the others, was pure white again.

"Yeah, itzmee." Paul shook his half-hooded head. "How'd you know?"

"You just showed me."

"Oh, shit, look." He turned towards Quaid, "Fire Ant remembered something he wanted to tell you, but couldn't find you so he told me in case I saw you. OK? He told me about a weird looking Brit looking for Maytag and Naldo, I heard about you and Freddy's tea party from some dock rats and knew things were going south when you didn't show up for your Deep Air on Tuesday. Quaid, it's a small town, you know that, man. A secret is like a guava and you can't hide a ripe guava, know what I mean, everybody knows everybody, right? So anyway, me and these wharf rats..."

"Hi, Miss Dimple Sue," the grinning wharf rats shuffled in unison and tried to look at her face.

"... geared up," Tall Paul frowned and continued, "to come find you and lordy, lordy look what we found. Need help?"

"We're good, thanks Navy," Quaid said. He nodded at Miguel and his crew and smiled. Dimple Sue nodded at Paul and his entourage and smiled. Everyone took a step back and then one of Paul's crew accidently triggered his paint ball gun. The red ball splatted on Dimple Sue's cut-off shorts, just above the fray. They were her work shorts.

Dimple Sue dropped her shorts. Tombolo dropped the boat hook, Quaid dropped the hose, Miguel dropped his helmet and the boys dropped their jaws.

"Let me see that hose, Quaid ... Quick! Quaid!"

A ruckus, unlike any ruckus anyone had ever seen, broke out as men raced to help Dimple Sue get the paint off her shorts. Misfired paint balls filled the air and hungry gulls screeched and swooped to eat them, later causing some inconvenience for several white Mercedes Benz owners. The smell of compressed gas billowed and someone yelled, "Medic!" Shiny baitfish leapt from the sea and frightened mullets maneuvered past a lurking manatee then dove, closer to the bottom.

Dramatic as it was, the opponents were too tired to rise to the occasion, and after Paul ensured Dimple Sue's safety, the SMAT team shuffled back to the van, stood in line to enter and departed.

Miguel and Quaid walked to a picnic table under the Gumbo limbo and sat down, face to face as the others gathered nearby.

"I say old chap, won't you kindly provide me with the stones and we shall bring this absurd and unpleasant incident to a dignified end, as gentlemen should."

"No."

BLACK STRAW

It would be a long night, or would have a been a long night except only minutes after Tall Paul departed, six more guys stepped out from behind a dumpster and semi-surrounded the group of already confused individuals. Dressed in civilian clothes including shirts and shoes and wearing mullet-proof vests an alphabet of agencies encircled them. No weapons were visible and everyone seemed calm as a man in a white smock with the letters NOAA printed on the pocket approached and extended his hand.

"Doctor Gorton Pimlico Blackstraw, NOAA advance team, at your service."

"Good heavens old son, Noah, that ark chap?" asked Miguel.

"No, NOAA, the National Oceanographic and Atmospheric Administration."

"Oh."

Quaid looked at Dimple Sue, "What are these guys doing here?"

Dimple Sue was tired. She shrugged her shoulders and stretched, "Dunno."

Dr. Blackstraw stopped in mid-sentence and tugged his smock closed.

Dimple Sue looked up, "Breathe everyone, breathe, in through the nose, out through the mouth ... or is it ..."

~ ~ ~

Although most of NOAA's work is open and available to the public, some projects remain classified. The NOAA

143

team, now in Key West, had received information from an unheard of organization called SATDATRATFLATPATIT.4.TAT.

The duty officer, Commander Lancaster Sudds, reported intercepting a top secret coded ping in the area of Key West. The signal was determined to be a high frequency pinger issued to the DEA. The DEA, in turn, had attached it to undercover asset (UA) 00-2, and if the instruments proved correct, the recovery team was within one mile of their most prized operative, a large American manatee known as Pong.

Pong, caught and tagged by NOAA five years ago, was fitted with a GPS and GoPro camera and was monitored as he made the annual migration up and down the coasts of Florida. Pong, of course, was unaware he had been tagged and only noticed a certain spot on his back always itched. He scratched it often.

Over the years, Pong was welcomed by almost every marina and Tiki bar from Jacksonville to Apalachicola but he was getting tired of lettuce or accidently ingesting discarded ketchup packets and condoms, they gave him gas and affected his buoyancy.

It was a long swim from Miami to Key West. Pong needed some R&R while in route and stopped to enjoy the fruitful canals of Cudjoe Key on the way towards Key West.

WHITE ROBED

On Second Avenue West, Pong found a shady spot along a canal wall where he could lip lock onto a slimy bulkhead, avoid getting run over by jet skis and enjoy a leisurely meal. He surfaced for some pre-grazing air and noticed a large human sitting in the shade of an old mango tree. The tall man, dressed in a long white robe with a white plastic colander on his head, held a dry martini in his hand and appeared unconcerned by Pong's presence as he sat watching a black and white TV on his seawall.

Pong approached slowly and after a few minutes of communal nose venting, the man turned the TV slightly towards the water. Together they watched the History channel, ate lettuce, vented and drank out of a garden hose.

Those were good days, but Pong eventually followed his instincts and after a good twenty-mile swim down Hawks Channel, cruised into the Southernmost Harbor to get a little strange.

As a manatee, Pong was not burdened by the old "mate for life" routine that others, like wolves, beavers and Catholics were cursed with. He was a free agent. He was his own manatee.

Pong's Pinger

Dimple Sue finished her languid stretch. Blackstraw adjusted his inseam and inhaled, "Recently, however, Pong's transmitter and camera failed and NOAA lost track of the mammal. We were deeply concerned until the trackers at SATDATRATFLATPATIT4TAT learned Pong's

Pinger had somehow re-activated and according to their calculations, Pong was in the Key West area!"

"Pong's Pinger? Bit of a wicket, what?" Miguel muttered.

Quaid stepped forward. "Look doctor, this is all very interesting but what do I, we, they and us have to do with it?"

"Well, we were hoping you would assist us in mounting a search for Pong," Blackstraw paused.

They ought to hire Maytag as bait, Beanne thought, and they ought not use the word mount. He wondered if it was the same manatee that humped Maytag in the harbor.

Miguel looked at Quaid and shook his head sideways.

Quaid turned toward Blackstraw, "Ok, listen Doc, we got some business to take care of and maybe then we can talk." Quaid said.

"Fine, we'll be back in the morning to discuss the details."

Six further confused individuals returned to the table beneath the gumbo limbo.

Pepe sat apart from Chi-Chi. Both felt inadequate and frustrated.

"This crap can't go on forever." Quaid said as he sat down. Let's make a deal right now. Look, we've got some stones, OK? Stones we almost died for, twice, OK? And, as far as the other assholes go, its best you don't know, so look Churchill, we've got a lot into this cluster fuck already and it isn't fair for you to demand *all* the stones."

"My dear fellow, fair is where one goes to see cows and eat corn dogs," Miguel said.

"Fair, is not blowing your coconut head off right now," Dimple Sue interrupted and produced a small .22 automatic from her cleavage. She found automatics were more comfortable than revolvers, at least in the tank-top tropics.

"Don't you get it pith-head, I'm tired, and Quaid's tired and so are Beanne and Bolo. Here's the deal, Mickey, we take 25 percent of the stones by weight and you get the rest. Sound OK to you, Quaid?"

"Yup."

"Billy?"

"Yup, that ought to work."

"Tombolo?"

"Yup."

"You good with that, Miguel?"

"Seems a bit lopsided, actually, let me instead suggest that I kill the bunch of you and take all the stones for the cartel?"

"Where are they?" Beanne asked Quaid.

Miguel looked up expectantly.

"If you're gonna kill Quaid, what are you gonna do it with, your accent?" Dimple Sue cracked.

Everyone hid a smile. "And, secondly, you'll never find the stones anyway, pith head, because no one knows where they are except Quaid," she added, "Right, Quaid?"

"Point well taken," Miguel said. Something is frequently better than nothing, he thought, and shook his head in agreement. *The way this mission had gone so far, and now that the FEDS are involved, it might be better for me to quit while I'm ahead.*

"Let us proceed," Miguel nodded at Pepe and Chi-Chi, "alone."

Quaid flipped a nod at Beanne, Bolo and Dimple Sue and whispered, "Meet me at the *Spooner.*"

Everyone nodded, exhaled and departed. Tension slipped away like a cheap hair piece in the rain.

Pepe and Chi-Chi headed for the van. Beanne, Tombolo and Dimple Sue headed toward the Spooner Wharf and, neutrally buoyant beneath *Betty's Boongy,*

Pong vented contentedly and settled to the bottom for a mud nap.

Miguel followed Quaid toward *Betty's Boongy* and down into the cabin. There may still be a chance to pinch the pebbles, he thought and adjusted his pith helmet to access a small syringe hidden in the carved out cork.

On the way to the *Spooner Wharf*, Dimple Sue slowed down and paused, "Hey, boys, I'm gonna stop home quick and pick up something. Tell Tall Paul I'll be in a little later, OK?"

"OK, Dimple Sue, see you at the *Spooner*," Beanne said. They watched her twerk into the darkness, while their eyeballs strained to abandon their sockets and follow.

"That's some woman there, Beanne," Tombolo said.

GONE

Just as Quaid pulled the stones out of his hiding place, the cabin door slammed and a marlin spike dropped thru the latch. Quaid turned and rammed the door with his shoulder and hurt it. He heard a familiar *FONK* sound and the cabin filled with CO2. Quaid held his breath as long as possible, hoped the concentration didn't reach more than two percent and then flopped to floor alongside the already flopped Miquel.

Minutes later, Quaid pulled into consciousness and rammed the door again. This time, however, the pin had been removed and he landed face first on the aft deck.

Quaid turned and crawled back into the cabin. Miguel coughed and opened his eyes; he seemed disoriented and unstable.

"I say, old bean, is this the type of thing you Yanks do all the time? Really rather tedious, you know."

"Listen, Churchill, if you don't shut u...

They both stopped, "Where are the stones?" Miquel asked and stood up unsteadily.

"Fucifiknow!" Quaid replied.

"I believe I am going to puke, old chap," Miguel rushed to the port side.

After a quick look around, Quaid spun on his heel and ran. He thought he heard a splash behind him as he left the dock, but kept going and raced toward the *Spooner.*

Quaid skidded to a stop near the bar, which in flip-flops is hard to do. He spotted Beanne and Bolo sitting at their regular shrimp-scented table, rushed over and sat down hard. Beanne slid a beer in front of him.

"What happened, Quaid?" Beanne and Bolo's expectant grins turned to dark eyes and furrowed brows.

"I got CO2'd in the *Boongy* and somebody came and took the stones while I was passed out."

"What about Miguel?"

"He hit the deck before me."

"Where is he now?"

For a moment Quaid recalled how disoriented Miguel seemed and remembered hearing a splash near the *Boongy,* but put it out of his mind.

"Dunno."

Silence, thicker than silt, overcame the trio.

"Where's Dimple Sue?" Quaid finally asked. The question hung in the air, like a bad smell on a hot night, suspended by six eyeballs looking toward the stars.

They looked away from each other and realized their faith had been misplaced, just like Quaid's t-shirt said, *"Confidence, the feeling you have before you understand what is really going on."*

"Fuck it" they said in unison, toasted with empty bottles, ordered another round and drank silently until the *Spooner* closed. A cold reality on a hot night, Dimple Sue was gone.

THEN AND NOW

Tombolo became disenchanted and took a job as a narrator on a manatee tour boat in Silver Springs.

Beanne couldn't afford another adventure and opened his own dive shop where he heard many great stories, but none ever sparked his imagination like the wreck of the *Faulty Dog*.

Naldo Cone left Miami, immigrated to Nicaragua and invented a combination love doll and air bed made out of native rubber. The highly touted "eco-hump" was picked up by Ikea and Cone lived happily, until deflation set in.

~ ~ ~

Although born to the sea and sand, the recent abuse suffered on or in the ocean demoralized Maytag. He'd slipped away from Quaid and his crew but did not want to return to Miami or a life of crime. Shortly after he faded into the bush, he went to Bonterra's hotel room. The door had been repaired with duct tape. A pigeon squawked and took a dump when Maytag entered. Although the room was paid for five more days Maytag couldn't stand the stench. He gathered anything of value including Bonterra's cash stash and the four bullets scattered around the base of the toilet bowl.

With enough money to sustain him for a short while, he spent several nights sleeping on the beach where he was disturbed by do-gooders and drunks who thought he was a beached manatee. A Fish and Wildlife Commission Officer arrived and advised Maytag to, "find another hole," and that same morning at dawn, the big fella found himself sitting in front of *Baby Rad's* diner.

There was something familiar about the joint, a sense of belonging.

Just before 6 AM, Moonbeam eclipsed the rising sun and spotted Maytag hunched on stool near the front door. She gave him the once over and fortunately, she was in a forgiving mood.

"Hey, Gordo, what happened to you, big fella? Ain't seen ya much. Ya know I didn't mean to hurt ya the other day, but I can get a little edgy now and then, ya know. Maybe it's 'cuz I don't get enough dick, who knows, ya know?"

The suffering Maytag looked up, compassion dusted with a hint of carnal desire poured from Moonbeam's early morning, small pink eyes.

"Hold your horses and sit right there," she said and unlocked the diner.

Maytag was unfamiliar with the term and pondered its meaning. Horses? Was she coyly referring to his *poki?* He only had one.

Meanwhile, Moonbeam scooped a handful of lard out of a can in the kitchen, returned to Maytag and rubbed virginal pig grease over the exposed and almost exposed parts of his sunburned, salt dried and sand papered body.

'You're rougher than a cob," she said gently.

"Ugga."

"Oh my!"

It was the first kindness, not to mention boner, he'd experienced since leaving his island home.

~ ~ ~

Pong, who would remain single the rest of his life, headed north and was forever lost by his NOAA trackers when the battery finally ran down. He flumbered out into Hawks Channel and returned to spend time with the White

Robed Man of Cudjoe Key. No matter how hard he swam he couldn't get going very fast, not that manatees are noted for speed. He arrived unusually tired.

When Pong reached Second Avenue the Robed Man, a mammal larger than Pong, was perched with Buddha like contentment on his seawall. He still sported the white colander on his head for both protection and ventilation and greeted Pong with a hearty nose vent. Pong responded with a series of special bubbles. The man stooped to remove a water-logged pith helmet with a small hole carved into the brim. It was hooked onto the antenna implanted in Pong's back. The Robed Man said nothing, stuck the helmet on a pole in the sand, like in *Lord of the Flies*, gathered the garden hose and grabbed some lettuce. Together the big ones listened to the unbounded, droning sameness of crickets, tinnitus, weed blowers and cable TV.

And still, on torpid evenings when the wind inhales, their quiet munching and contented venting lend a salty serenity to an otherwise frenetic paradise.

A THIN INVITATION

The shock of losing the emeralds, not to mention Dimple Sue, faded like cheap house paint and Quaid's life returned to near-normal.

Sometimes, life on this orbiting dirt ball called earth reminded him of a roulette wheel. When young, he thought, we whirl around the rim at the speed of life, then the wheel slows and we drop into a random slot, a random grave, to win for some, lose for others and remain captive until the wheel stops spinning.

Quaid returned from a towing job in the Marquesas and stopped at the *Spooner* for a Tuesday drink. He took a stool at the bar.

"Hey, Navy, how about a Deep Air?"

"You gotta go down ..." Paul quipped.

"But you don't gotta come up ..." Quaid finished and they laughed as survivors often do.

"You got it Army. How ya doing, man? You took a couple hard licks didn't ya?

Oh hey, I almost forgot, there's a letter here for you, come about a week ago, sorry."

"Really, huh, let me see it."

Paul scratched around under the bar and handed over a plain white envelope.

Too Quaid Butler
C/O the Spooner Wharf Bar
Key West, Florida
Earth

There was no return address. Quaid opened the letter, tossed the envelope onto the bar and unfolded a blank sheet of paper. He looked closely and discovered one long blonde hair nestled in the fold. He held the golden fiber to the wind. It streamed out and pointed west.

Paul returned with Quaid's drink, "Who's it from?"

Quaid hid the hair, "Not sure."

Tall Paul picked up the envelope, sniffed it and looked closely. "There's no return address or anything, but there's a postmark on the stamp, reads ..." he held a shot glass to his good eye to magnify the print, "all it says is ... O ... Odessa, Texas."

Quaid leaned back, usually a bad idea on a stool and took a deep breath. It was the kind of deep air he liked best nowadays.

He dropped the hair, recovered his balance, picked up the envelope, finished his drink and nodded at Paul.

"Be seeing you, Navy." Quaid gave a small grin, left a big tip and walked out.

He was tired of the ocean anyway.

ONE WAY ONLY

Three days, 1800 miles and five gallant Greyhound buses yielded a corridor of time for quiet reckoning. During half-awake glances through the bottom of his delaminating safety glass window, Quaid Butler noticed the earth's curvature appeared to be reversed, and as he sank lower in the diesel-powered pew, the view through the blue tinted corner of the glass gave the impression they were traveling away from earth.

Like tiny kamikazes, fearless interstate flies dive bombed lost or unprotected morsels of food while Quaid rested easy in the corner of his seat and reflected on the last few months of love, loss and deep air.

He fell asleep at 55 MPH with his mind open and his mouth shut. Days on a bus were, he noticed, twice as long as other days.

On the way west of the Mississippi, small children constantly vented, "*el viento del grano,*" (wind of the bean) with the innocent enthusiasm and similar capacity of giant blue whales.

The timeworn bus had one flat tire in the rear, but the driver pushed on towards Odessa anyway. Nine tires would be enough the driver had decided. The overheated rubber ring flapped noisily, like someone spanking a pumpkin, alongside its brothers. Useless, but as in many families, still along for the ride.

On a Texas highway of unending sameness, Quaid recalled his grandma's advice, advice delivered many times, over many years. "Listen to me you little shit," her ancient speech, now a gravely garble in a far-flung dream, filled the anxious space between his ears, "the *best* things, the *right* things will come easy, boy, they'll find you if you're good, so don't worry, be hap..."

Granny's voice usually trailed off at this point in the lecture when she hiked up her house coat and began dancing around the retirement home. She'd gone into the Lazy Bones rest home at age 62 in order to, as she put it, "Get a good seat."

He turned to face his mirrored likeness in the kaleidoscopic glass. He'd always tried to be good, but in some folk's eyes, he was always being bad. Like all of us, he could be both. He hoped Granny was right and stared at the unraveling ribbon of highway through his own reflected image. Looking out and looking back through himself at the same time he wondered, am I coming or am I going? It was hard to tell, but the moment reminded Quaid of a poem a friend had written.

I saw myself in the rearview mirror,
two cars back, on a scooter. I looked tired.
OBJECT IN MIRROR ARE CLOSER THAN THEY
APPEAR

MUST TURN RIGHT a sign read, an arrow pointed
and we did.
I looked again, I was three cars back,
ingested by a python of steel.

Heading west, my hairs faced east

as if longing to remain. I fanned the follicles
and hoped
to find myself again
in that prism to the past,
in the rearview mirror.

Quaid sighed, momentarily fogging the glass like a Nasograph in the old sinus commercials. The sigh reminded him of many other sighs and no matter the circumstance, he reflected, when it comes time to exhale the weirdness, one sigh fits all.

Fractured white lines bled into one and black asphalt smiled as the sun passed behind a cloud that looked like Albert Einstein's hair.

Below the window, someone had scratched the words, *"I AINT A REDNECK... I'M A SCARLET FUCKIN NAPE!"*

~ ~ ~

Greyhound bus #444 slowed on her approach to the West Texas bus terminal. Lethal stench from an overflowing toilet and muffled gagging filled the crowded cabin. The 1965, silver-sided Scenic-Cruiser had been rolling for seven hours straight as her nine, thin, road weary tires careened across an old oil stain that resembled a flattened brown body. The blemish had existed for years, but continued to startle new drivers on their first run to Odessa.

"Urban road kill," the veteran drivers joked.

A rusted ONE WAY ONLY sign with a bullet hole through the black arrow, stood at the entrance to the terminal. An abandoned bicycle, rust dusted and missing a wheel, lay chained to its base.

Most of the passengers could not read English, but all knew the meaning of ONE WAY ONLY, it was the way of their lives.

#444 creaked to a stop at the depot gate where slip-streamed desert dust and oily diesel smoke billowed forward to engulf and season the new arrivals. #444 belched her cargo of poor, disheveled, but apparently happy, plant-picking people onto the station platform then idled impatiently, always in search of new highways to devour.

Small families chattered, took deep breaths of the much fresher air, gathered their meager bags and moved quietly onto the ever-flat land, blending like sand on sand paper. The sight of poor, but apparently happy people interested Quaid. People who should be worried about everything didn't appear to be worried about anything and their laughter came as easy as their breath. The fertile earth was both their master and savior.

"You can depend on the earth, it is our life, it is our grave," the old ones said, "She will be here long after man has passed."

But who, Quaid wondered, would fill the last hole.

ODESSA

After five days, showering in sinks and smelling like the air from a cheap pool toy, Quaid Butler exited the bus and flipped a small duffle bag over his shoulder. It landed on the head of a Lilliputian passenger behind him who said nothing, smiled and moved on.

At least one foot taller and fifty pounds heavier than anyone around him, Quaid enjoyed a Gulliver perspective.

Waiting for his luggage to be thrown on the ground, Quaid pulled out a crumpled brochure about Odessa he'd found in a malodorous seat pocket.

Odessa *was founded in 1881 as a water stop and cattle-shipping point on the Texas and Pacific Railway.*

The first post office opened in 1885. It was incorporated as a city in 1927, after oil was discovered on the Connell Ranch southwest of Odessa.

The jack rabbit is the symbol of Odessa. Beginning in 1932, Odessa held a rodeo for roping rabbits. In one legendary competition, a cowgirl named Grace Hendricks roped a rabbit from horseback in five seconds and beat her male competitors. The rabbit roping rodeo ended in 1977, the result of objections from the local Humane Society, but many businesses and residences around Odessa proudly display models of heroic and unusually elongated jack rabbits to this day.

Odessa was mentioned in James Michener's Texas as a city where "you are more likely to be murdered ... than in any other city in the nation."

Well, that's good information Quaid thought and turned to the map where he found the last two map pages stuck together with a wad of gum. He tossed the pamphlet into a waste basket made of woven tumbleweed and noticed he was alone.

In the quietness of the platform, Quaid rolled his eyes, shook his head and sighed when he remembered, he didn't have any luggage.

MOSEY ALONG

Ector County Deputy Dimple Sue Pankersley knew herself well enough to know she didn't know herself very well. How much comfort she drew from that understanding is also unknown. She knew she was good looking, but didn't know why. She knew she was smart, but didn't know why. She knew she was lonely, but this one she was close to figuring out.

Odessa is even worse than it was when I was here last; she said to herself in a half dream as she dressed for work. A dry Texas wind stirred the fresh smelling cotton curtains in her small apartment. Bugs moseyed back and forth on the window sill. It was too dry to fly.

As usual, she started the morning with a positive thought,

"You know, some of these cowboys can't seem to figure it out... crime-don't-pay... and it **positively** don't, unless a'course, you go about it in a legal manner."

She stood, stretched and strapped on her gun belt, then paused with a sheepish grin and coyly dropped the belt in order to don her regulation Kevlar panties. Safety first.

For a moment, Dimple Sue remembered the recent good times in Key West; times before things got all mixed up with the "nothing but bad luck" emeralds. She recalled how she did what she had to do, when she had to do it, to save her friends, Quaid Butler, Billy Beanne and Tombolo, not to mention her own dang self. Other times, after a drink or two, she recalled the kick-ass-free-fall sensation of burning her ex-boyfriend, Bernie's boat in the back waters off Key West. The memory of the forgiving sea helped humidify her dehydrated soul.

But now, it was time for work. Deputy Pankersley finished dressing, hopped into her patrol car and headed into town.

NO ONE LEFT TO LOVE IN TEXAS

Dimple Sue knew she was in a "mood" this day and always thought of Key West when she needed a smile, but her desert dried lips hurt so badly she had to stop and that, unfortunately, irked the deputy.

Deputy Pankersley paused in the shade of the *Krazy 8's* pool hall and adjusted her ten pound gun belt. "Damn thing is dragging my ass down," she griped.

Pankersley had the noon to night patrol. She tossed her sun-bleached blond hair and allowed the desert air to caress her neck. It hurried to do so, while super-heated atmosphere rippled off the pavement like slow rolling Caribbean swells and uncertain figures loomed in the billowing heat waves.

Her brief repose was interrupted by a determined West Texas dirt fly. The cheeky hexapod made the mistake of landing on her exposed and seemingly vulnerable neck, and although no one could fault the fly's taste in women, his joy was short-lived when a lightning fast, leathery hand with emerald- green fingernails sent him down the tubes to eternity.

"Guess I've gone back to sheriff'ing for a while," she said to the plummeting fly. "I need some brain time to ponder on things and a cop, 'specially a cop with a gun and an attitude, can take all the time she needs for thinking. Am I right on that one, Buzz?"

The fly made no attempt to respond and embraced the sizzling pavement with a hiss.

The stolen emeralds she'd taken from the boys in Key West laid heavy on Dimple Sue's conscience. She knew she wasn't the first one to steal them, shit, they might have been stolen five or six times before she took them, but the thought did little to calm her.

The "Green Devils," she called them, were hidden in the loamy dirt behind her apartment in Notrees, a small town northwest of Odessa. She'd tried to bury them in the yard below her bedroom window, but the ground was as hard as her mother's homemade bagels. Instead, she was forced to dig up her landlord's dog grave behind the house in the dark of night and hide the stones under the restful mutt. A small wooden cross tilted near the dirt mound, the name *Dazee* scratched into the sunburnt wood.

And now, after taking the emeralds, skipping Key West, leaving her potential lover and working two months at her old job as a deputy sheriff in Ector County, her previously soft and supple tropical skin was dryer than old bones, her hands rough as a cob, hair straight as a fence post and her lips constantly chapped. She licked them frequently, giving a false impression to wishful observers, while making the problem even worse.

The only good thing about Texas, she noted, was her gun didn't rust as fast. She was embarrassed to think that was the only positive thing she had to say about her current life. But, let's face it...there was just no one left to love in

Texas. Her sparse family of one aunt and two half-brothers were long gone, as was her dad, Dancin' Don Pankersley.

Guess I shoulda wrote something to somebody, sometime, somewhere, somehow ...

Another thought, however, gave Dimple Sue encouragement. It was the hope her cryptic message made it to Key West and Quaid Butler was on the way to find her. She didn't know why she was so set on being with him, but she was.

Then, Deputy Pankersly did what she always did when stressed, she checked her gun. A quick metallic spin flashed six brass bullets; ass out in the chamber, ready for their solo dance of death. It was a tool with only one purpose. She loved charging the gun, it felt like she was loading history and knew that any one of those babies could save her life or take someone else's. A quick snap of the wrist, the cylinder clicked home and she was good to go. It was one of only a few revolvers with a custom laser sight. She was reminded of an old sniper saying, "You can run, but you'll only die tired."

"I know I'm still young," she mumbled and adjusted her gun belt, "but damn son, trying to stay that way is getting old fast."

With the blind courage of a land crab crossing a freeway, Deputy Dimple Sue Pankersley stepped off the curb and into her shadow.

A hundred feet from the pool hall, Deputy Pankersley paused to watch a shabby man, his back towards the street, hands hidden in front of his pants, apparently preparing to take an unlawful whiz on a taxpayer-funded prickly cactus growing near the curb. With a practiced move, she approached silently; paying no attention to the four cars that screeched to a stop. She spun the perp in an involuntary pirouette and locked his arm behind his back in the process. A cell phone bounced and skittered in pieces across the pavement and settled near discarded pamphlet advertising free sand.

The elder perp showed no resistance and squinted over his free shoulder.

Dimple Sue was in a foul mood and knew instantly she'd probably screwed up. The guy turned his back to shade his damn cell phone! Duh! He probably held it down low because his eyes are bad. Duh! She leaned around and snapped a quick peek at his fly, zipped! Duh!

"Damn!" She released the perp with a reverse pirouette.

"Excuse me officer, but what's happening here?"

"Oops. Sorry sir, just a little misunderstanding on my part, OK."

"What about my phone?" he rubbed his shoulder where Dimple Sue had grabbed him.

Dimple Sue drew down on the whiney perp and shot him between the fucking red-rimmed eyes...Bang!

Of course, it was only the dream of an instant, but helped quiet her guilt induced nervousness and reoccurring bad mood. What Dimple Sue considered a, "bad mood," most folks found downright frightening and would head for their root cellars or scrunch down on the floor of their car and lock the doors.

"How may I hep you, sir?" Deputy Pankersley asked and fondled the Taser accessorizing her right buttock.

The perp's eyes, she noticed, seemed good enough to spot the Taser and he never took his eyes off it, except to glance at her badge.

"Oh, ah, that's OK," the perp leaned forward to get a closer look at her badge. He would be one of only a handful of men that would live to tell the tale, "Okay Miss Dep-Pooty number 36B, guess I'll just mosey along."

With that, the petulant perp gathered the pieces of his flip phone and as promised, moseyed along.

STORIES OF THE
OLD WURST

Quaid caught a ride from the bus station into town with a Halliburton oil rig worker. The pickup truck smelled like gun oil, cheese burgers, fading hope and methane gas. An almost hairless rabbit's foot dangled from the rear view mirror. He asked to be taken to a Best Western Motel; he knew they were available most everywhere.

"Where ya from?" the roughneck asked and floored the Ford.

"KeyW- West," Quaid replied as his head bounced off the head rest.

"Huh, that's where all them pickle smokers is from, right?"

Although Quaid had never heard the term, it was pretty obvious what the roughneck was asking.

"Well, there's a lot of fish smokers down there too, I call tell you that."

The roughneck created a visual and decided it was better not to respond. Instead, he rolled own his window and spit into the wind. That didn't go well either.

~ ~ ~

After a twenty-minute ride, the rig worker pulled over, said howdy-do and dropped him off. Quaid nodded a howdy-do and looked up.

Above his head, a shabby neon *Wurst Western Motel* sign flashed like a street walker's smile. With a shrug of his lanky shoulders, Quaid entered the lobby and checked in and after a quick howdy-do, walked down the sidewalk to room #413.

Quaid inserted a key into the door lock. A thermometer screwed into the wall nearby read, 102. A plastic, battery powered bass, mounted on the back of the door, squelched out a friendly, "Howdy-do."

The room itself was furnished like a burrow or perhaps an art deco lair. A small bed with a rabbit motif duvet, wedged itself against the bunny wallpapered wall near the window. Rabbit themed pillows were scattered about. A faded picture of a smiling rabbit, held vertically by its front legs and wearing a blue ribbon, hung crookedly above the flaccid mattress and a bowl of something that smelled like mints, but looked like rabbit pellets, lurked below.

Instinctively, Quaid moved to correct the maladjusted picture. The frame slipped from his grasp and landed on the bed. And there, like piss holes in the snow, two dark-eyed bullet holes stared back from the dirty drywall. The bullets had missed the wall mounted AC unit by less than eight inches.

"Well," Quaid reached to re-hang the picture, "that's good news." He flipped the AC onto HIGH COOL and headed for the commode.

A rabbit paw chandelier hung above the sink, the shower had plastic rabbit paw handles and the toilet paper was fuzzy. Rabbit breeding magazines with colorful cottontail centerfolds lay next to the bowl which was also shaped like a bunny. The user flushed it by reaching between his or her legs and pushing on its nose.

After brushing his teeth, for an instant they looked like rabbit teeth, he stopped at the front desk and asked, after a quick howdy-do, for directions to the nearest saloon. "Yup, you'll be wanting Jack's Rabbit Saloon, just down the road apiece," the pretty, buck-toothed desk clerk advised. She twiddled her pen between her long fingers slowly and went on to tell him that the *Wurst Western* was owned by a wealthy German couple who didn't speak English, had not studied advertising and claimed to serve the only authentic *Bratwurst und Knockwurst* west of Pennsylvania.

"I'll be riding this here desk 'till nine, cowboy. Let's have us a rodeo!"

She smiled at his foot wear and winked a howdy-do.

DOWN THE
RABBIT WHOLE

It was a short, flat, flip-flop journey of four blocks to *Jack's Rabbit Saloon.*

The saloon's faded wooden door opened with a loud creak and welcomed Quaid into a cool, dark West Texas bar room filled with mostly silent men smoking hand-rolled cigarettes. Leaning on their elbows, they stared at the acrid smoke rings as though the nicotine expulsions were storm clouds forming in a small sky.

One pilgrim did not have his elbows propped on the worn bar; instead he was face down on it, arms dangling at his side, an unlit cigarette hanging from his lips. Someone had put his cowboy hat over his face to keep the dust off, while overhead a well- populated fly strip spun slowly beneath a ceiling fan. Only one set of flailing bug legs showed any motivation to escape. The others were serene, or dead.

Bad way to go, Quaid thought and nodded at the doomed, but still flailing fly. He pulled up a stool as the bartender arrived.

"Howdy-do," the bartender smiled out one side of his mouth.

"Howdy-do. Nice town you got here," Quaid responded.

"Yeah, it is if you like dirt, oil, lackanooky and horse shit." The barkeep waved his soiled rag at a niggling dirt fly.

"Well, I'm used to bullshit, does that count?"

"Looks like you come to the right place, son." The bowlegged barkeep slipped a grin, took the fly out with a quick snap and nodded at the beer cans lining the back wall of the bar. All but three read, "COME and TAKE IT" Lone Star Bottling Company.

Quaid ordered and the barkeep moved toward the cooler.

A cold cold one slid to stop in front of Quaid, "What does, 'Come and Take It' mean?" Quaid asked.

"It arises from an old Texas motto that caught on during the Battle of Gonzales, back in 1835, the first battle of the Texas revolution. We kicked butt on that one."

"Sounds Texan, alright," Quaid burped.

After a couple cold ones, Quaid realized he didn't have much to go on when it came to finding Dimple Sue. He'd looked through a phone book in the motel room but found no Pankersley's listed.

Quaid's third Lone Star slid sinuously down the bar and nuzzled to a stop in his wrinkled, pre-formed hand. "Nice slide."

"Nice catch," the barkeep replied.

He took a swig and wondered if he had been foolish to abandon his life in Key West, not to mention his boat and his friends, for a single blond hair and a postmark. But, he had to admit, it was a sexy message and anyway there was no reason to involve his crew in this mess. Plus, who said anything about abandoning anything; his was simply undertaking a hastened departure to avoid an unpleasant circumstance, like getting shot. He knew his mates Beanne and Bolo would watch after themselves and his salvage boat, *Betty's Boongy*, for a while.

Dimple Sue had come and gone so fast that, combined with the emeralds mess, she'd never told him anything about her family or her past and he hadn't asked. All he knew is what she showed him with her eyes and thighs and that alone was enough to bring him on up to Texas. He also knew she probably took the emeralds, but preferred to focus on his sensual memories, at least for the time being.

Quaid hoisted his empty bottle, drank some air and stared at the fly-specked mirror behind the bar. He noticed an unusually long-necked jack rabbit head mounted on the wall above, its beady glass bunny eyes stared at eternal nothingness.

Quaid winked at his long-necked bottle, "Howdy-do, I'm wearing flip-flops in Texas and my Lone Star is lonely tonight. Come and Take It! Yee haw!"

The drunker he got the more the other patrons looked like rabbits, the Cheese Doodles were the color of carrots and everyone was sniffing.

The barkeep hopped over, "You ready for another cold one, partner?"

"Don't do if I mind," was Quaid's dyslectic response.

The bartender shook his head then returned, set a fresh one down and wiped the wet Olympic circles left by Quaid's previous bottles. The bar rag slipped and Quaid noticed the man was missing three fingers on his right hand.

"Tough to hold that rag, eh? Just curious, but what happened to your fingers?" Quaid nodded at the barkeep's right hand sporting only a thumb and middle finger.

"Rabid rabbit, sumbitch bit me to the bone and kept biting. I was doing a little friendly roping in my corral outback. That little hopper didn't take to it, I guess."

"Damn. What happened to the rabbit?" Quaid inquired.

Without looking, the barkeep nodded backwards towards the wall, winked, but said nothing.

"Hell of a neck on that rabbit, partner," Quaid remarked.

"Yup, dang horse pulled up short, mighta set him off, hard to tell what a rabbit's thinking."

Quaid finished another cold one. "I'll bet it is. What's your name, partner?"

"Rales, Garvan Rales."

"Nice to meet you Rales, I'm Quaid Butler."

"Howiffy..." Garvan took a moment to re-seat his dentures with his thumb, "Damn desert air wreaks havoc on the gum glue. Howdy, Quad."

"It's Quaid."

"Got it."

"Hey, Rales, on another note, I know it's probably a long shot, but..."

"That's OK, Quad I'm used to it, that's all there is out here, long shots." He repeated Quaid's name again like professional bartenders everywhere. "There's as many stupid answers as they is questions, seems you can learn as much from a bad example as you can from a good one, am I right, Quad?"

"Ah, I guess, anyway, I read there are around 100,000 people in this town and... here comes the stupid part...did you ever hear of somebody called Dimple Sue?"

"Dimple Sue Pankersley?"

"Yeah, I think so." How many Dimple Sue's could there be?

"Dimple Sue Pankersley, oh hell yeah, I think they used to call her, *Miss Spanky,* until she taught some boys not to use the word"... Rales rolled his eyes, "Oh hell yes, them Pankersley's was around these parts for years, all growed up and gone now though. You ain't never heard of Dancin' Don Pankersley?"

"Nope, just got into town, rode the bus up from Key West."

"You like to square dance?" Rales asked with a twinkle and slid another long-neck down the bar.

"Never tried it." Quaid wondered if he had mistaken the nature of the bar, or Rales' intent.

"Well look, I've never met this woman, Dimple Sue, but I think she's Dancin' Don's daughter. I heard she was a deputy sheriff here some years ago. They say some guys got arrested just so they could get frisked by her and others got ticketed for staring at her badge too long. "*Too much respect,*" she wrote on their tickets. Get my drift? Anyways, let me tell you about ol' Dancin' Don, it was sad what they done to him."

Quaid burped politely, stood up, flexed his buttocks and shifted his weight onto his elbows like the other synchronized drinkers. Damn flat-butt syndrome follows me wherever I go. He sighed, took a swig and glanced up at the long-necked rabbit's beady eyes. He saw one wink.

Rales continued, "See, Don was an oil rig worker, a chain-man. He took the risky job of wrapping the spinning drill shaft with chain. Turns out he was so fast the crew nicknamed him Dancin' Don. He was damn good at his job. Well then, after a few years he got married, had a couple kids and took up square dancing. Later, I believe it was around the time his daughter, Dimple Sue, was born'd that he became a square dance caller at the *Best Western*. He learnt it from a record. Guy was smart as paint and for a while, Dancin' Don was pretty famous around these parts."

Quaid relaxed.

"Then some Germans come to town, bought the old *Best Western Motel,* turned it into the *Wurst Western Motel.* Naming a motel after a danged wiener is pretty weird in my book. Anyway, the *Best Western* was where Don used to call out square dances on Saturday nights, but them Huns went and changed the style of movement from square dancing to *polka*, whatever the hell that is. Well, Dancin' Don tried his dangdest to convert his square dance calling to suit the polka folks, but it just didn't catch on. There was dosey- doen' and single hand *Molinets* and sash-shayin' and Bohemian national pivot an' free spins an' swingin' yer partner an' folks crashing into each and every other every-damn-where's. It was a righteous mess on the dance floor, lemme tell ya..." Garvan Rales took a breath and went on. "Well, Dancin' Don got depressed, who could blame him, he left town and took all them Pankersley's with him. I ain't heard the name Pankersley in quite a few years. His daughter must be in her thirty's by now."

"Damn, Rales, that's quite a story." Quaid held his empty bottle up to his eye like telescope. "You wouldn't happen to know how I could find this Dimple Sue, would you."

"Lemme ask Big Burl, our dishwasher, he's washed most everybody's dishes around these parts."

Another eager Lone Star sashayed down the bar as Rales hollered toward the kitchen, "Burl! Get your ass out here."

That's weird, Quaid thought, the first person I ask knows of Dimple Sue. Is that a good or a bad?

A double action kitchen door swung open and a set of massive denim clad buttocks formed a wedge and then pushed thru the opening. Slowly, Burl Wetwood came into view. He was a colossal man and had to pass backwards thru most doors. If he tried to go thru face first, his belly massed up and blocked the opening and his thick alligator arms were too short to reach the door frame to help pull his ownself through. His once white apron was wet and stained and looked like a grimy cape on a medicine ball. Finally, Burl popped thru the door, turned and approached Quaid. When he leaned on the bar it creaked.

"Boy's here about Dimple Sue Pankersley, right Quad?" Rales looked at Burl then Quaid.

Quaid nodded.

"What is it you got to do with Miss Pankersley?" Burl asked with narrow eyes.

Having planned on asking the first question, Quaid was momentarily stumped.

"Ah..." It was an abrupt, disquieting, but nonetheless fair question.

Burl turned towards Rales, "Dudes' weird."

"Yeah, he's from Key West," Rales replied softly.

"Oh, you need say no more." They watched quietly while Quaid slipped into his mind.

What *are* my intentions? Quaid thought. Damn, maybe I should have spent more time thinking about why I'm doing this and less time staring out the window at the world. The bus trip was like watching an old cowboy movie, I felt like I was a part of America for a while, the velocity made me feel like I was doing something, even when I wasn't.

Anyway, here I am, doing what I always do, acting first and thinking later, and except for the emeralds, losing Dimple Sue and probably being chased by bad guys who want to kill me, it's worked so far. So what is it, fear, love, greed that's got me sitting here in Bumfuck, Texas?

Dying would be an inconvenience, sure, but it was something he had accepted long ago in a muddy hole in a muddy land. He'd led a team of six men, working off the grid in the boonies, but all members agreed there were seven on the team. Death, they said, was the 7th man. They called death, D-man, and he followed them like a shadow dog. The team understood D-man might be the only one left to care for their smoldering souls and accepted him as an equal as they went about the business of war.

Where did that shit come from, he asked himself, then shook it off, took an optimistic slug from his always half-full bottle and continued his internal conversation punctuated by a series of Lone Star burps. No point in thinking about changing horses' mid-stream, he supposed, especially when you have only one horse. That one cracked him up. He soon concluded his self-evaluation along with his N'th beer and satisfied, turned to face Burl Wetwood, dishwasher.

"OK, Mr. Wetwood," Quaid took an long oxygenating breath, "I appreciate you asking me that question, because, like Mark Twain said when facing a difficult inquiry and I quote, 'I was pleased to be able to respond rapidly. I said... I don't know.' That's what he said."

Rales and Wetwood harmonized a tonal, "Hunh?"

Quaid sensed he had his choir and that this conversation might lead somewhere, but before he could continue, Wetwood broke in.

"Call me Burl," Wetwood said, "So, what kinda business are you in anyway, mister...?"

"Butler, Quaid Butler."

"OK, Quad."

"It's Quaid."

"Got it."

"Anyway, I was, still might be, in the marine salvage business."

"Marine salvage, huh...what's that?"

"Well, according to Captain Black Bart Bartholomew, Navy Salvage," Quaid warmed to his story,

"Marine salvage is a science of vague assumptions based on debatable figures taken from inconclusive experiments and performed with instruments of problematic accuracy by persons of doubtful reliability and questionable mentality."

"Sounds like my life," Rales said.

Wetwood eyeballed Rales and whispered, "Sounds like my wife's cooking," then quietly aside, "This boy can talk, Garvan, sign of intelligence ya know, talking."

Wetwood turned toward Quaid, "I used to work down in Key Weird in the eighties at a Titty bar called the Naked Bunch, heard of it? Well, anyway it was a freak show with sunscreen, is what it was. Most ever'body was too slippery to get a grip on real life."

"Real life, huh," Rales snarfed, "real life like living in this oversized, bullet-ridden, rabbit-assed, oil-stained litter box?"

" 'Fraid so, Rales, fraid so ..." Wetwood turned to Quaid. "What was it we were talking about, Quad?"

"I was saying how much I appreciate you boys trying to help me and I'm hoping ya'll can tell me where I might find Miss Dimple Sue."

"She a friend of yours?"

"Yup, maybe more than that."

"Does she know you come out here to find her?"

"I believe she does. She sent me a message."

"What was the message?" Rales chimed in.

"A hair."

"A hair... I see ... You like beer, Quad?" Wetwood asked.

"Well, I liked the last how many's and I ain't about to change my opinion at this point in time, how about another round, Marvin?"

"It's Garvan."

"Got it."

The day turned dark as sweet crude oil and the room became a shadow as some men looked for hope through the bottom of their bottle and night raced west to eat another day.

RACE FOR
THE BOWL

Quaid awoke with the wickedest headache in a long time. He smelled burning methane gas and hoped it wasn't him. Peering through a rabbit hole in his hangover, the bunny-ish room came into focus and his previously happy herd of Lone Star beers now bellowed loudly and gathered for the roundup.

Finally untangled from the sodden sheets, Quaid fumbled to the bathroom, dropped to his knees and hugged the commode. However, because it was shaped like a rabbit, every time he leaned over to hurl, he hit the nose with his belly and it flushed.

I can see the headlines in the Odessa Burr now, *Quaid Butler, deep sea diver. Got sea sick in a toilet bowl and damn near drowned.*

Quaid remembered last night the way a fish remembers the sea when it's laying on the beach after the tide goes out.

After opening his desert-dry eyes, Quaid realized he'd never undressed. That'll save a few minutes, he thought. He grabbed a toothbrush, squirted some tooth paste on his tongue and put an open bottle of water in his pocket. He found his polarized sunglasses, took a second pair from his duffle bag, put them over the first pair then hopped towards the door. The only thing he remembered from the night before was he had to go back to the saloon in the morning and it seemed it was still morning until he stepped out the door and inhaled 98 degrees of desert day. He was late.

Walking as briskly as possible with only one flip flop , he wondered if he was unconsciously snapping back, like some men do after a good fight or fuck, back to where it happened, not quite sure why, empty of adrenalin and knowing it will never be the same again, no matter what.

Fortunately, it was neither of the "f" words, simply a vague, but powerful memory that drove him to return to Jack's *Rabbit Saloon* to get a little, as his dad used to say, "Hair of the dog that bit you." He was anxious to find what he'd forgotten.

Jack's Rabbit Saloon looked like a drained aquarium tank in the light of a West Texas day. Even with two pair of sunglasses, the room was too bright for Quaid and most of the other fish-eyed patrons. He looked down and noticed his water bottle had leaked in his pocket. Shit.

Garvan Rales wiped the bar top, "Afternoon, Quad."

"Garvan, man, that rag is making too much noise, how about a little, "Hair of the dog?""

"You ate the dog, Quad. What you need is a prairie oyster!" Rales said with a grin.

"What the heck is that? Anyway, what did you tell me last night, I forget?"

"Well now, ain't that an awkward position to find your own drunk-ass self in, eh?"

Quaid pulled both pairs of sunglasses down low on his nose and looked up to plea for mercy, but caught the rabbit's glassy-eyed stare instead. It hit him hard in the equilibrium department and with a hand cupped over his mouth, Quaid Butler, deep sea diver, raced for the poop chute.

At least there's a urinal in there so I won't have to bend over as far, he thought.

Still woozy, he was nonetheless pleased with his common sense approach and sprinkling of gallows humor as he plunged face first into a white ceramic cubicle, grabbed the flush lever and prayed to whatever god would have him. There must be at least one, he thought and pulled the lever.

"Watch your head," Rales hollered and reached for a mop as Burl Wetwood entered, ass first, through the front door.

"Seen that fella Quad what was in here last night?' he looked at Rales, "Boy sure could talk...and drink. How's our Lone Star inventory?" Burl asked over his shoulder.

"Low, Burl, real low. Quad just poured back in, had to make a run for the bowl, probably hurling by now. That boy needs a prairie oyster."

"Huh, not surprised...rabbit set him off, didn't it? Watch yer head, Quad!" Burl hollered towards the toilet. The orbish man rotated and moved toward the kitchen to embark on his second ass-first approach to another day.

Like a tourist admiring the royal guards at Buckingham Palace, Rales paused respectfully to observe Burl's daily butt breach.

Burl Wetwood, dishwasher, pivoted, acknowledged the challenge with a nod, exhaled and went for it.

That must get old, Rales thought as the building creaked and he returned to his midday mopping.

NEXUS IN TEXAS

If Quaid hadn't mistaken the Sani-Cake in the urinal for soap, he would have returned to the bar room much sooner and felt much better about himself.

Rales paused and wrinkled his nose, "You look flushed, Quad. You remember what Burl told you last night?"

Quaid dropped into a chair like a sack of mulch, "I thought I've made it pretty clear that I don't, Rales."

"Well, you got about five minutes to remember or you won't need to and Quad, wipe your drunk -ass face!"

Quaid did as instructed, then dropped a handful of pukrified bar napkins and turned when he heard the familiar creaking of the front door. This morning, however, it sounded more like a hull plank giving way on an old wooden sailing ship at sea.

DIMPLE SUE

Two pairs of sun glasses slid down Quaid's aquiline nose and slammed to a stop on his quivering nostrils. Rales shaded his eyes as the saloon door sailed open to frame the dusky silhouette of Deputy Dimple Sue Pankersley. Desperate paparazzi sun rays fought to fill the space around her like a body halo. She looked like Clint Eastwood with tits.

"Hey, Quaid."

"Dimple Sue!"

"Someone said you might be here," she glanced toward the kitchen.

"Yeah, I'm about as here as I can get. Am I under arrest?"

"Not yet, honey, but you look rough and you stink, what the heck you been doing, Quaid?" Dimple Sue asked.

"Maybe we should get a table," Quaid stood quickly, too quickly it appeared. His last memory was of Dimple Sue's practical tactical shoes as he hit the saw dust covered floor, his descent cushioned only by the soft blanket of unconsciousness.

"He likes me," she explained to Rales as they propped Quaid up against a bar stool.

"I can see why," Rales smiled. His mouth looked like a old piano keyboard. After a moment he stood, nodded and walked away to tend the other bleak-eyed survivors.

"Dih, duh, Dimple Sue... is that you?" Quaid mumbled through shrunken lips and red-rimmed eyes.

"Yes, it's me baby, you found me! Besides, who else has lips like these and carries a gun?" She engulfed him in a firm, non-motherly, embrace. "Maybe we should get a room, instead."

This is too easy. I like it; he thought, pushed her gold badge out of his face and fell into her warm, West Texas arms.

Deputy Pankersley cradled Quaid's head and began humming, "He flies through the air with greatest of ease, the daring..." while Garvan Rale's spinning mop watched longingly from the dance floor.

FACE FIRST

Quaid awoke to find himself scrunched, face-first, in the crack of a dusty, well-worn vinyl car seat. He propped himself up on one elbow and looked out the back window.

"They coulda put me in right-side up," he complained and watched the West Texas dust billow behind, then follow and strain to engulf him, like a rogue wave in the Gulf Stream.

It took painful effort to roll over and face forward without tumbling onto the empty ammo boxes, bulletproof vests and empty doughnut bags littering the floor of the police car. Dimple Sue's flashing blond hair flared in the wind and Quaid was about to call her name when he ingested an arbitrary dirt fly. His profound gagging caused Dimple Sue to look in the rear view mirror.

"Quaid, honey, you OK?"

"Ack..gorf...hoof...hoof!"

"OK then, that's good, but lemme know if you're gonna die, otherwise there's a shooting out to the old Spyvey spread and I got to get there, Pronto! Hang on."

Although he heard the words, "Pronto, Hang on!" Quaid's body, as well as his brain, did not react in a timely fashion and both were slammed backwards against the seat by the Crown Vic's rapid acceleration. The impact, however, worked to expel the confused hexapod from the back of Quaid's throat and into Dimple Sue's thrashing corn silk hair. He could smell her sweet scent and again thought about saying something, but it was hard to hear, let alone speak at 90 MPH with the windows open and the siren on. It didn't seem like the right time anyway.

Quaid fell out of consciousness again and wondered when he'd last heard the word, *Pronto.*

THE LIVILY
SPYVEY'S

The sound of a shotgun blast, followed by the passenger side window exploding inward awoke Quaid. He kept his head down and listened as the dust and smoke cleared. He was alone. The driver's door was open and no Dimple Sue in sight.

After a few seconds he heard, "Oops, sorry folks, you kinda caught me off my guard there."

An old man, in dirty overalls and wearing a, "I'M BUM FARTO," t-shirt stepped out of a nearby bush, a smoking double barrel shotgun in his hands. He squinted, puffed out his sunken lips and looked around to see if anyone was listening.

'That's OK, sir." Dimple Sue said and stepped out of an adjacent bush. She put a red laser *bindi* between the old man's clouded eyes, "You one of the Spyvey clan?"

"Yep, it's pronounced Spy-vey, like ivy."

"You mind pointing that gun away from me, sir. " Dimple Sue asked, although it wasn't a question.

"Nope, don't mind at all," he said and stuck the smoking barrel in the dirt, "dang thing gets heavy."

Dimple Sue holstered her gun. She glanced at the cruiser then focused on the geezer, "We got a call there was some shooting going on out here."

"Well, yeah, you most likely did, me and the missus was out target practicing."

"Target practicing, eh, on what?"

"Each other mostly, don't need a license for it in this state, ya know. It's just something we do to keep the old love light burning, keep the old flame alive, good exercise, running for your life in the bush. Gets the juices flowing , I'll tell ya, but like I said, I had one shell left when you come up in a cloud of dust and spooked me, thought it might be Ivy, that's my wife, trying to take me out with our old Ford Pinto. Ha, ha!" The old man had no front teeth, his laughter sounded like a camel's nuzzing.

Dimple Sue looked over her shoulder towards the perforated cruiser and spied Quaid's curious face peering out the window from the rear seat. No blood visible. She winked and turned back towards old man Spyvey.

"Where is your wife, sir?"

"Don't know for sure, mighta winged her back near the crick." Spyvey nodded towards a downhill path.

"You know, sir, it's a strange kinda love that takes up with shooting at each other, don't cha?" Dimple Sue said.

"Yup, may seem like it to some, but... well...all love is kinda strange, ain't it, Missy?"

Dimple Sue emabulated on the concept, then cuffed the geezer and frog marched Spyvey to the Crown Vic where she opened the back door, flashed a smile at Quaid and said, "Scooch over honey, we got us a prisoner."

Deputy Pankersley pushed old man Spyvey into the back seat, slammed the door and headed down the path towards the creek. She was getting, "that feeling" again and wished she was with Quaid in the back seat instead this old back-woods geezer.

In the rear seat, the two men looked at each other briefly and then turned away without speaking.

Fifty feet down the path, Dimple Sue noticed bright blood on the ground and further on saw a small woman hunched over in the weeds. There was a slight movement.

She's alive! Dimple Sue rushed towards the woman.

"Howdy, missy," the old lady said as Dimple Sue skidded to a stop.

"Mam, are you alright?"

"Yup," the woman looked up, a bloody skinning knife in hand, "That old man Spyvey missed me again, took out a danged possum instead." She held the still squirming rodent above her head.

"Sometimes, I think he misses me on purpose...used to get me pretty regular in the old days." She stood and hoisted her housecoat with one hand to reveal a set of well-preserved, pellet- pocked buttocks, then sat down gingerly.

"Believe me now? He says them pocks help, "break the suction," whatever the hell that is. Might be his eyes are going bad, but I swear, if I didn't have a nice ass, I don't believe he'd see me at all."

Mama Spyvey pointed at the still wriggling possum. "Want some, missy? She's a fresh'un."

The conversation had drifted too far afield to suit Deputy Pankersly. She drew her .38, and blew the half-skinned mammal into fleshy forest confetti.

Her bad mood was back.

"Get up."

Dimple Sue frog-marched the stunned Mama Spyvey uphill to the patrol car. She jerked the old man out of the back seat, winked at Quaid, hauled both of the Wild West weirdoes into the house and hand cuffed them to a heavy pipe near the toilet bowl.

Dimple Sue grabbed the old man's lower lip, jerked up and out and with no teeth to interfere, dropped the small handcuff key down the back of his throat. Spyvey swallowed it before he knew what happened.

"Drink lots of water," the deputy said, flushed once for good luck and walked out the door.

Dimple Sue returned to the patrol car and noticed Quaid was missing. A rotating glance found him standing in a bush with his back towards her, taking a whiz.

She approached silently. "Drop it and put your hands up!" she commanded.

Quaid, too tired to be surprised, shook and responded, "If I do it'll get sand on it."

They both laughed and climbed into the back seat for a quick reunion. Adrenalin will do that to a person.

After the earth took a breath and they returned from a place where there is no time, Dimple Sue swept the remnants of the shattered window off the front seat.

"What did you do with those folks?" Quaid asked.

Not one to admit to her cleverness, Dimple Sue replied, "Nothing much, just told the old man he should try and give a shit."

She could hear the old Spyvey's laughing like idiots as they drove away.

Now, **that's love,** she thought.

Even though Quaid was forced to pick small shards of glass out of his ass every time they hit a bump, he found the front seat far more comfortable than the back. With the passenger window absent, desert air roared through the patrol car like a blow dryer at a car wash. The more he looked at the desert, the flatter it got and although it was too loud to ask, he knew where they were going. Even the thirsty desert air could not stop fine beads of sweat from forming on Dimple Sue's upper lip. He stared at her lips, she smiled at his eyes.

It was going on 6 o'clock when Deputy Pankersley radioed in to advise she was finished for the day.

A RECKONING

The sun emptied like pancake mix on a sandy griddle and spread across the waffled horizon as they arrived at Dimple Sue's apartment in Notrees.

It was time for a reckoning, Quaid reckoned and thought about Dimple Sue and their time together in Key West, his home turf. Now, he was out in the flat Texas bush and did not feel at home or particularly useful on her turf. Decision one: Get back to Key West.

Dimple Sue was in a hurry. Dry humping in the patrol car, she called it the *Texas Tango,* combined with the Spyvey's obvious passion, the smell of gunpowder and blood, had got her all riled up. Deputy Pankersley slowed her Crown Vic from 30 to 0 within ten feet and scruffeled to a side-ways stop next to her apartment. It took a moment for the dust to settle before they could find the front door. Her apartment was small, but tidy and the smell of fresh laundry, gun oil, beef jerky and *Shalimar* perfume loitered in the eager air.

They looked at each other and for an instant, considered behaving like adults, but both had seen what that can lead to and headed for the bedroom instead.

"First things first," they said at the same time and laughed

"Well, here we are, Quaid." Dimple Sue hooked her fingers in her gun belt. "I guess we need to do some talking, but before we do," she held up one finger and pointed, "you go wash up while I run down to the store and get us a little

Texas Tea and some food. You like Lone Star?" she
grinned.

"Think I proved my love of the Lone Star last night,"
Quaid replied.

Dimple Sue put a Bob Dylan CD in the machine and
hit play. "You're a scootin' hooter," she said, "I'll be right
back, Q-ball."

Dimple Sue was in a loving mood. She checked her
gun and slipped out the door singing along with Bob:

> *"It's a never-ending battle for a*
> *peace that's always torn,*
> *Come in, she said, I'll give you,*
> *shelter from the storm."*

"Q ball?" Quaid looked out the bedroom window as
he shed his flip flop. A row of white panties hung from a
clothesline like erotic flags of surrender. He spotted a small
dog grave nearby. Graves made him sleepy.

Least they have enough dirt to bury in here, he
thought, can't bury anything bigger than a beagle in Key
West without it popping up after a few months. He stared
at the small cross planted in dry earth, the word *Dazee* was
carved in the weathered cross beam.

He turned from the window and headed for the shower.

"Probably best to let her have her way with me," he said
softly, "show some manners. I'll have to get serious about
this situation sometime, but why here, why now?"

A romantic of the first water, Quaid shed his two day
old shirt, dropped trou' and reached for the shower knob.
Even the water felt dry.

Quaid emerged from the bathroom sniffing his armpit to find Dimple Sue frying baloney in the kitchen. Two cold Lone Stars condensed in unison on the counter.

"Well," Quaid said and dropped his towel, knowing he'd slipped into another better smelling world, a place away from forever miles, ugly bad guys and endless circular contemplation.

"I hope this is a dumb question, Dimple Sue, but you do have the stones...don't you."

"Is a bear's asshole watertight?"

Quaid was quiet. Dimple Sue was not good with analogies. It was supposed to be a "frog's asshole,"... anyway, "I guess that's good," Quaid finally said, "but in a way, I wanted them stones to be gone so we wouldn't have our lives screwed up again."

"Don't worry Baby Cakes; we got the law on our side now."

"What do you mean?"

"I mean, I'm the law out here. You think those goofballs in Miami are gonna come out here? How would they know where we're at? You know, I took them stones for your own good, don't cha?"

She had, as she hoped, explained her reason for leaving before Quaid could ask.

"Anyway, don't worry, I'll show you where they are after we eat and wrestle," Dimple Sue said. For some reason, she felt safe when she was with Quaid. It was weird, she thought, they'd hardly said anything of consequence to each other in their few months together and yet it seemed she'd been with him forever.

"Wrestle?" Quaid finished his sandwich in one bite.

BADGER

Sherriff Rally Badger rocked back in his wooden swivel chair and rested his well-worn cowboy boots on a large manila envelope. The move resulted in his feet being higher than his head. This additional extension gave him a twinge in his lower back, but he paid no attention and smiled at the slow-moving ceiling fan slicing the desert air.

For over 30 years, Rally Badger had been a sheriff in Texas and spent most of it in the northwest corner around Odessa. He'd tried to retire for years, but even if he figured in his pension, he would never have enough money to live the way he wanted. Betting on cards, cars, horses and women left claw marks on his bank account. Sure, he'd got a few hundred bucks in bribes now and then and a blow job here and there, but nothing to get excited about. "Can't live on blow jobs alone," he always said. Yet here in his office, confirming his longstanding suspicion of random occurrence, he found his boots resting on more money than his ass ever had. A bag of cold, hard cash stared back at him.

A few hours earlier, a short dark man wearing a flowered shirt, red shorts, a gold Rolex and flip flops had walked in and dropped the sack on Badger's desk, along with a picture. The man spoke briefly, wrote his contact number on Badger's Dunkin' doughnut wrapper and left.

All Rally Badger had to do, according to the dark stranger was, "Keep eye out for deez gringo and call me, eez family beezness, si, no, eh."

The stranger went on to say the guy was an *estupido gringo* named, Quaid Butler.

Guess I'll put Deputy Pankersley on this one, Badger thought, she's a looker and still got some energy left in her plus, I sure could use the money.

Badger called his bookie.

STARK SNAKED

Morning always arrives without invitation and this one was no different. In the early light, drained of everything but air, (air doesn't drain,) Quaid lay on his back with his arms above his head. Dimple Sue curled like an inchworm beside him. It was good and getting better. He knew he would eventually have to make a move and unfortunately, within minutes of awakening, his eventually turned into NOW.

The desert around Notrees was flat and dry; elsewhere in the state, it was dry and flat. Thru the bedroom window he watched as the sun flashed the moon and both fell full upon the ever level desert sea. Only one lone cactus, that looked like an upturned middle finger, broke the membrane between air and earth. Quaid had stopped thinking about the emeralds during his pursuit of Dimple Sue now, however, they were together and faced the same problem, again, what to do with the stones.

After a night of what Dimple Sue called, bedroom rodeo, the lovers looked like they'd been throw'd against a wall by a brahma bull and liked it. After a good night, there is not much to say, or much that needs saying. Quaid got up and looked around for something to wear while Dimple Sue made coffee.

They took their black coffees, stepped outside and walked through the backyard towards Dazee's grave. A Western Diamond Back rattlesnake lay curled pensively on the small dirt mound. Its tail twitched spasmodically as they approached. Dimple Sue was barefoot and wearing a gingham house dress, so was Quaid, although his was the more conservative of the two. Neither had a weapon so, with silence born of understanding, they prepared to back away from the nasty reptile.

They hadn't moved a foot when Dazee's final resting place exploded in a billow of red fleshy dirt. The deafening roar made them cover their ears. When the dust cleared, Dazee's cross was completely gone as was the snake. Only a smoking hole and the peppered remnants of an old dog body remained.

The roar had emanated from an antique double barrel shot gun held by a skinny man who approached in Yoga pants tucked into oversized cowboy boots. A wooden duck call hung from a nipple ring on his right teat.

"Howdy, Miss Deputy Pankersly, hope you don't mind I took that Texas worm for a ride to the great snake hole in the sky."

Dimple Sue was stunned, but quickly regained her composure.

"Why, Buddy Earl Mousehill, is that you? No, Buddy Earl, I mean no, not upset at all, thank you, nice shot. I was just telling my friend Quaid about you."

Buddy Earl looked at Quaid in the housedress, shook his head, but said nothing. Dimple Sue continued, "We came out here to pay respects to Dazee and look what happened. I am truly sorry."

"Indeed it is me, Missy, ol' Buddy Earl his ownself, and it ain't your fault that critter chose this place to die and anyway, how are you this fine morning, if I may inquire?"

"I'm fine, Buddy Earl, but it's a shame about Dazee's grave, here let me help fix it," Dimple Sue said and solemnly began to kick sticky red dirt back into the hole. Didn't know a snake had so much blood, she thought to herself. She could see the black Kevlar bag starting to poke out below the dried dog cadaver.

"Why that's mighty kind of you Dimple Sue, you know how much that dog meant to me, don't cha?"

"I do, Buddy Earl, she means a lot to me too."

"Well, ain't that nice, and since I've had to bury her four times already 'cause of the wind erosion and such, I believe I'll leave it to you and your, "girlfriend," he winked at Quaid, "and go take a whiz."

With that, Buddy Earl Mousehill pivoted on his boot heels and headed down the path to his nearby house.

"Looks like Buddy Earl likes to tell it like it is," Quaid smiled.

After checking Buddy Earl's progress, Dimple Sue knelt down, flipped the desiccated dog and grabbed the dusty bag below.

"Does crazy follow you everywhere, Quaid Butler?" She laughed, finished kicking dirt into the hole then turned and hugged him fiercely.

The blood spattered house dresses billowed and gently caressed their bodies as the lovers returned to the apartment.

ON THE JOB

After hiding the emeralds in her underwear drawer and a brief, but lustful skirmish near the coat rack, Deputy Pankersley readied herself for work. She checked her gun while putting on makeup and soon the pair boarded her dusty patrol car and headed towards Odessa. Without saying anything Dimple Sue let Quaid know she wanted him to stay with her in Notrees. With a peck and a promise, she dropped him off at the Wurst Western to gather his things, then turned east and headed for the sheriff's office.

"Morning, Deputy Pankersley," Sheriff Rally Badger said over his elevated cowboy boots. There was dung on his desk.

"Morning, Sheriff," she said to his worn leather soles. "Doesn't sitting on your coccyx all day long hurt your back, Sherriff?"

Badger had no idea what coccyx meant, "No, but thanks for asking, I'm fine."

After last night, Dimple Sue needed some time to get her head back into law enforcement. Don't want to be walking around, grinning like an idiot, when you're dealing with leftover drunks, she reminded herself.

"Deputy Pankersley, please come over here for a moment."

Badger was always profoundly polite to Dimple Sue and would've a licked thousand postage stamps just to be near her. But, he knew she was a package he'd never open.

"Got us a little business to attend to and I was hoping you might help me with it. Fella came in here a while ago, didn't speak English too good and asked me to keep an eye out for some drifter knowed as Butler, Quaid Butler. "

Badger held up a Xerox copy of a newspaper clipping that showed Quaid and another man sitting on the bow of a sunken shrimp boat in Key West.

Damn.

"Anyway, this fella reckons he might be around these parts, said he needs to speak to him about a family matter, although he don't look like family to me. You mind putting the word out, see what you can come up with, I'd sure appreciate it. Make some copies and pass them out to the boys. Seemed like a nice fellow and I always try to help good people, it's my job, ya know." Dimple Sue knew Badger never did anything for nothing.

Dimple Sue's standard issue panties wadded, they were supposed to be the *Anti-Wad* type, her buttocks clenched and wrinkled her allegedly *Wrinkle- Free* uniform pants and to top it off, her throat turned dryer than a molted snake skin. Reminded of an old saying, "I started out with nothing and I still got most of it left," she checked her gun and put her brain in gear. Damn those stinking stones.

"I'll see what I can do, Sherriff." Dimple Sue took the picture, turned and walked out of the office, leaving Badger to contemplate a heretofore unobserved set of wrinkles.

Being blindsided, however, did not disturb Dimple Sue's equilibrium. She was used to tough times and hard choices and this was just another one in a long string of unintended fuck-ups she would eventually un-fuck.

"I'll never be a sniffer," she mumbled to herself.

Dimple Sue was referring to sniffer dogs. Sniffer dogs were people who, in her opinion, followed the scent left by those actually doing something. The sniffers always arrived just after the party ended.

Dimple Sue stopped then returned to Badger's office, "Sheriff, my patrol car isn't working right and I wondered if I could use one of our unmarked cars while the mechanics look at mine?"

"You betcha, Dimple Sue, just keep me informed."

Dimple Sue signed out a beige Ford sedan and wasted no time getting back to Quaid, but drove calmly, as if she somehow knew this day would come.

THE RUN

The unmarked car made record time to the Wurst Western, skidded to a stop in a four-wheel drift and disappeared into the now predicable billowing dust ball. When it cleared, Quaid was waiting and ready to go.

"Get in and gear up, Quaid, we gotta run!" Dimple Sue paused long enough to show him the picture. "Badger gave it to me, wants me to look around for some drifter named Quaid Butler. Where did he get this damn picture?"

"Ah ..."

"Think about it, Mister Drifter. I got to get home and pack and we gotta mosey along. Pronto. Make a plan, will you."

Quaid flopped into the car, buckled up and held on.

After a fast trip to Notrees, Dimple Sue ran into her apartment and gathered priority items, defoliant, make - up brushes, bullets and her prize underwear including a pair of *Agent Provocateur* buffed black silk panties with Velcro bullet pouch. She turned and pulled the dusty, blood specked Kevlar bag out a drawer, transferred the stones into a lip stick bag and wrapped them in the aforementioned panties. This precious bundle found a home in the bottom of her small hard-sided cardboard suitcase; it was easy to run with. The rest went into her larger Samsonite Stryde-Glider Spinner suitcase. She gently placed a picture of her dad, Dancin' Don Pankersley on top of the panties and closed the suitcases, took a quick look around, threw a library book at a scorpion lurking near the refrigerator and slammed the front door. The mail box fell of the wall.

Well, I brought out more than I took in, she thought; guess that's a good sign.

Dimple Sue tossed two suit cases and a bag of ammo into the trunk, climbed into the driver's seat and presented the picture again. "Damn, what a mess. You got a plan yet, Quaid?"

"Ah ..."

Dimple Sue said nothing more and headed north.

After 50 miles of silence, Dimple Sue asked, "Are you thinking, yet?"

"I'm trying to, but we're going so fast my ideas are getting sucked out of my ears."

"You're not thinking. So, let's get you to where you can, baby cakes." Dimple Sue smiled and floored the Ford. Not that there was much flooring left to do. "But listen; don't worry too much, because no matter how fast we travel, we're just one step ahead of the past."

That thought kept Quaid's mind busy for a while and they didn't say much during the 400 mile run for survival. Piss, pump and pass were all they did. They took turns driving for 2 hours at 80 MPH and since the AC was broken and the windows down, it would have been difficult to chat anyway.

Dimple Sue eventually tired. She knew they couldn't hide forever. A hungry realist, she skidded to a halt at a weathered stop sign near Chickasha, a small, remote town 20 miles south of Oklahoma City.

Dimple Sue turned to Quaid, "Are you thinking yet, Quaid?"

"Yup."

"No, you're not."

"Am too, but maybe I can think better if a take a whiz, a whiz I should have taken 50- miles ago.

"Yeah, good idea Quaid, I could use a quick whiz myself...and some food!" Dimple Sue replied and pulled onto the shoulder of the road.

There was not another vehicle in sight as the two exited the car and moseyed towards the setting sun. Two-hundred feet from the highway's edge, the beige sedan blended with the mushroom colored desert beyond.

Being lovers on an upward trajectory both were careful not to spoil the mood with domestic indifference and veered slightly away from each other and into the nearby scrub brush.

Both squatted in their respective locations. Dimple Sue because she had to. Quaid, steeped in chivalry, crouched because he was tall and could see through the scraggly brush if he stood.

Quaid was the first to feel it, a slight tremor and a deep throaty vibration, consistent and getting stronger. Dimple Sue felt it as well and they both rotated, still in full squat position, towards the oncoming specter. Two glaring white eyes stared back at them through the scrub and grew increasingly larger as the vibration increased. It quickly became obvious that the source of the thrumming was two freight trailers pulled by a dusty white semi-tractor. The big rig must've been traveling at a high rate of speed, since it took less than a minute to travel from the horizon to the four way stop signs only 200 feet away from those who were in search of relief.

BOONE GANDER

In the truck cab, Boone Gander was tired, not only tired, but sick and tired and not only sick and tired, but upset to a point of illness due to the mind -numbing stench of two trailers full of hogs on the way to El Paso for slaughter. He particularly hated the small towns, their predicable speed traps and other civic impeachments that slowed his transit. At several crossings he, as well as local commuters, were overtaken by the billowing reekage of seventy-five premium, but fearful hogs which stenchified the surrounding area with the most porcine of perfumes.

Hence, when Boone was on the open road he kept his speed up, ensuring it was always more than enough to suck the hog-stink into his diesel scented wake. If Boone hadn't been trying to change his contact lenses while driving, he might've been more attentive to the highway. Unfortunately, after dropping the right lens on his left cowboy boot then reaching down to retrieve it, he did not and could not notice the beige car parked near the stop sign.

When Boone looked up, all he saw were his headlights reflecting in a pair of red tail lights, less than 100 feet in front of his rig. With reflexes born of too much coffee and not enough sleep, Gander swerved to avoid the automobile. He later recalled doing about 60 miles an hour. With screeching tires, the big tractor and two trailers jackknifed and swept down the highway sideways like a giant steel squeegee. The ventilated trailers, their coverings held together by flimsy aluminum and cheap wood, caught the outer wheels and flipped on their sides. The cab and Boone followed. The last trailer caught the sedan and engulfed it in dust, anguished iron, shattered glass and squealing pigs.

Pigs are tough cookies; none of the squealing porkers was injured badly. Once the conglomeration of machinery quit sliding and screeched to a stop, the rotund beasties scurried out through the fractured roof of the trailer, took a dump and surveyed their new surroundings.

Pigs are always hungry and out behind the wreckage of the car, from which a strong scent of gasoline emanated, one little piggy sniffed some of the items thrown from Quaid and Dimple Sue's luggage. The car was mangled badly and the trunk had popped open spreading their belongings across the desolate highway.

Quaid had not intended to make a Baby Ruth, but he did. Dimple Sue was ominously silent. Still, after a few minutes, both had rummaged enough fibrous material, while scuffling about in the full-squat position, to tidy up their involuntary response to the fearful scene.

They stood and surveyed the area in time to see pigs rummaging through their clothing and toiletries. One little piggy spied a small object wrapped in black cloth that had been thrown from a broken suitcase. The black cloth was surrounded by three bags of cellophane-wrapped beef jerky. Pigs are not picky and true to form, one of the smaller one-hundred pound gluttons managed to ingest all three jerkies and Dimple Sue's special panties in one gulp.

The pig, not into feminine under garments, was further piqued when he attempted to chew the stones. Stones of any type gave him gas. He swallowed with an irritated, "Oink."

"My panties! He ate my freaking panties. You Pig! What's that smell?" she called out. One of her two suitcases had broken open, the other, a Samsonite *Stryde Glider Spinner* was predictably undamaged. Dimple Sue began gathering a few necessities strewn across the hot pavement, including her favorite black Spandex cocktail dress. She fanned her nose, did a quick inventory and quickly stuffed important items in the always roomy, *Stryde Glider*. Then, she pulled her gun and set her red laser dot on the porcine purloiner who stood nearby snuffling for something more palatable to ingest. She tensioned the trigger, but quickly realized the possible consequences of her action. The pig became living luggage.

Dimple Sue, familiar with animals of all types, including human, moved quietly and calmly toward the porker. After several light caresses she turned smoothly, slipped the cocktail dress over the pigs head, put its front feet through the armholes and twisted the remaining four-feet of sequined Spandex into a serviceable leash.

Quaid was still removing burrs from his butt and having trouble focusing when Dimple Sue emerged from the wreckage with a pig on a leash and a gun in her hand.

Not one vehicle had passed in the last twenty minutes.

Before Quaid could fully absorb the situation, his attention was drawn to his left where a small bow-legged figure emerged from behind the rubble. Apparently, the truck driver had escaped out the passenger side of the cab.

He'd been alerted to their presence when he heard a piercing cry from the other side of the mess, "My panties!"

The driver was relieved not to have killed anyone or anything, as far as he knew. He was intrigued by the current situation. With him he carried a bottle of tequila inone hand and a smoking Virginia Slim cigarette in the other.

"Howdy, name's Gander, Boone Gander," the driver said as he wobbled towards Quaid and Dimple Sue.

"Howdy, I'm Ed Bland and this is Miss Suzy Tibbs."

Quaid saw no reason to give any factual information at this point and under these circumstances. They had to become ghosts, for a while.

"Nice to meet cha, folks," Boone stepped forward to shake hands. He glanced at the pig and Dimple Sue's gun, but said nothing. However, he still held the Virginia Slim clenched between his gnarled fingers. With one last toke, Gander flipped the butt away and reached for Quaid's hand.

The handshake had not been consummated before the seeping gasoline ignited and the entire steel and rubber mechanical macramé was engulfed in flame. It would be a long time before the car could be identified, Quaid thought, as the spilled gasoline ignited the leaking diesel fuel.

Within minutes Dimple Sue's bag of ammo started cooking off. Most of the pigs had already distanced themselves from the mess and were lost to the gathering darkness, all except the one porker who stood leaning comfortably against Dimple Sue's tanned legs. She held the leash lightly and said, "Well, this sucks," as a stray bullet stirred the dirt near her feet.

As they backed away from the fire, Gander commented, "Dang missy, hope you don't mind me saying, but that pig looks mighty good in black! Glad none of em' died though, that's one bad smell when they cook off, I can tell ya. Yes sir'ee Bob."

Well, one thing led to another and soon they were squatting on dirt mounds just far enough away from the fire to still feel its heat. The night was cold. None had fully recovered from the recent incident and the bottle of tequila was more than two thirds gone when Boone Gander, tired of the pig's incessant snuffling, poured the remaining tequila down its throat.

"That ought to do'er," Boone said and lit another Virginia Slim.

Twenty minutes later a lone pickup truck entered the intersection and stopped. The owner stepped around the truck and started speaking on a cell phone. Boone stood slowly, then headed towards the man, "I'll check him out," Gander said.

PIGGY BACK

"We can't stay here, Quaid. You know they're going to come looking for us, don't cha?"

"I know, Dimple, pretty soon they'll be firemen and cops all over this desert disaster."

Dimple Sue looked at the sleeping pig, then up at Quaid. "You got a knife."

"What?"

"The pig ate the stones. Guess I forgot to tell you, sorry."

For all the nasty situations Quaid had been in, the idea of gutting a live pig, even for stolen emeralds, just did not sit well.

Before he could respond, Dimple Sue said, "Just kidding, honey bun. But really, Quaid, what are we going to do now?"

"Well, we walk and we take the pig with us. So wake him up and let's go. By the way, that's a clever leash, Miss Pankersley!" Quaid knew there was no point in dwelling on one's misfortune. Look for the humor, he reminded himself, it will keep you sane and there is plenty of it in any shit storm.

"Thanks, I've always been good at practical fashion," she replied with a dusty twerk.

Their gentle pokes turned into sincere prods in an attempt to wake the napping guzzler. The pig was plastered.

"Thanks, Boone," Dimple Sue muttered. "Okay, Quaid, let's take my *Stryde Glider*, strap the panty eater on it and get away from here till we can figure out what to do. Give me your belt."

WHEN PIGS FLY

Before Earl Gander returned, if he did, they'd strapped the porker to the tough Samsonite *Stryde-Glider Spinner* and rolled it into the hard packed, endlessly same brown scrub brush. Quaid returned every few yards and dusted over their tracks with a piece of tumbleweed.

Within an hour they could hear the sounds of machinery working to clear the highway. By then they had dragged the pickled pig over half a mile, during which it farted like a truck backfire every time they hit a bump. Quaid hoped the porcine crepitation's wouldn't give them away. He mentioned his concern to Dimple Sue.

"Quaid, get your hat on straight, desert dog. What kind of hero is going to sniff the wind and go chasing after pig farts in the desert?"

Good point. Maybe it was time to rest.

KEY WEST BIGHT

A manatee sucks a seawall, screeching birds dive-bomb dead fish, outboard motors fart oily winds on fishermen so wrapped in UV swaddling they look like mummies with sunglasses. Along the docks, live-bait netters fetch up cigarette butts and condoms along with fresh mullet; garbage trucks wreak a cacophonous stench, charter boat mates entice with pictures of scantily clad women holding dead fish, muffler-less mopeds mope all while pious church bells drone amidst the shrill clatter of empty glass booze bottles tumbling to their shattered destiny in a dank green dumpster.

Only these sounds disturb the stillness of a Sunday morning in Key West Harbor.

Like a barnacle clinging to a bulkhead, the Spooner Wharf bar clung to the south side of Key West Bight. The dockside watering hole awoke with the temperament of a recently hibernated bear; ready to eat fresh green money, guzzle warm whiskey and drink blood-red wine.

Budward "Bud" Moon III, floor care consultant at the Spooner Wharf bar, paused to allow patrons who had stayed the night, perhaps involuntarily, to gather their things and move from under the warped and aromatic picnic tables, tables where a million bivalves had crossed over.

It was 0700 and the "Breakfast Club" was assembling. Only hours before they had been the "Last Call Club."

Drunks are tough folk, Budward Moon mused. Maybe I should write a self-help book called, "How to be a Drunk without Drinking," might get famous, who knows? This random thought was swept away with the first stroke of his beer-smelling broom.

The rousted inebriants nodded their appreciation with awkward weaving movements. Budward Moon watched them walk and felt sea sick. The inebriants clustered loosely at the edge of the warped dock. Early, oily, water distorted their haggard, hung-over faces, but no one noticed, for ugliness is a given in the world of the eternal drunk. Instead, each stared at the still water and took the measure of the other. It was a new day, there was drinking to be done and one should always take the pulse of one's competition. In odd, but practiced unison, the dedicated imbibers blithely cast aside last night's excesses and readied their souls and livers for the grand imagination of another day, a day when anything could happen but, they grudgingly acknowledged, rarely did.

After freshening up with a convenient garden hose, drying off with handfuls of purloined toilet paper and each other's clothing, the herd of ambulatory hang-overs, The Breakfast Club, returned to take up their stations at the bar. Since the Spooner Wharf had only one enclosed side it was, technically speaking, always open. The Clubster's claimed their respective stools, stools still warm from the night before. They arranged their elbows in military fashion and then, in random uniformity, raised one crooked index finger and waved white cocktail napkins like small flags of singular surrender.

'Let's talk about what we're gonna do, instead of what we done..." one grizzled geezer offered to ignite the day's first meaningless conversation.

"Yeah, but every time we **do** something, it instantly becomes something we **done**... Gotta act fast just to keep it current, right?" We're just a nano-second away from being history at any given moment, right?" one wise ass quipped.

JOEY DA' LIP

The peripatetic philosopher looked two stools down at his toothless comrade, Joey da' Lip, and rubbed his forefinger and thumb together in the universal monetary gesture.

"Lip, my man, you still got any money left over from selling that picture of you and Quaid?" the aforementioned geezer asked.

"Ah, um, you betcha, Red Rider," Joey da' Lip replied. He was flabbergasted that his business dealings were already common knowledge on the water front. After all, he'd taken precautions against being found to be a snitch, he'd even done the deal in the men's room with the light out for fuck's sake! Still, there was always something to be salvaged from any wreck and like they say, "Once you lose your reputation, life becomes much simpler." Joey da' Lip, always one to enjoy the limelight having money brings, countered with a call out to the bartender, "Paul, old pal! Give us drinks all around! Let the drunkards drink!"

Joey da' Lip had once worked for Quaid Butler and his Slow Boat Towing and Salvage Company. A few years ago, in the good days, he was working a salvage job with Quaid when a local newspaper photographer offered to take a picture of them sitting on the outrigger of a sunken shrimp boat named LUCKY. He gave both men a copy of the picture.

Da' Lip was a good man on deck and took chances no one else would, but the demands of maintaining his qualifications as a professional fool finally caught up with him and he got fired.

On the last mad scramble for a salvage job, he'd been so drunk; he reported for duty, then stepped off the dock onto Betty's Boongie... just after the vessel had left the wharf. Damn near drowned. It was embarrassing and Quaid fired him on the spot.

A week ago, a Cubanish fellow had been hanging around the Spooner Wharf bar asking if anyone had a picture of Quaid Butler. Guy said he owed Quaid money and was trying to find him, so when the Cuban offered a reward for a picture of Quaid, Jimmy da' Lip, still stinging from his damp dismissal, sold the tattered photo. He'd dug the rolled-up photo, stored in a non-lubricated condom, out of his shorts, handed it to the dude and pocketed a wad of damp *dinero*.

In the seventies, the Spooner Wharf had been a clearing house for lost souls, vagabonds, men, women and other blends who arrived to turn over another rock in their quest for the end of their particular rainbow. Somehow, those wind-blown souls knew that when you live on the other side of sunrise, everyone can find someone they've never met... but have always known.

It was 0745. Some desires never rest.

IN THE BUSH

It had been a long night in the bush, who knew Oklahoma could be so cold. Quaid preferred Key West, where even your coffee never gets cold.

The pig had remained docile throughout the night and several sleeping arrangements were attempted and discarded. In the end, Dimple Sue awoke to find herself curled up between the pigs back and Quaid's belly, a tri-spoon arrangement. During the night, Dimple Sue covered the pig's bristly back, first with the remaining section of her cocktail dress, which she intended to donate to the porker and then with blue jeans and other dense materials to reduce the prickly discomfort.

Daylight delivered an improved perspective of the surrounding area. Across the ever- flat land, Quaid was able to see a narrow gravel road running almost parallel to the highway. They were only a few hundred yards from the road where, Quaid noted, dragging the pig would be easier. The *Stryde Glider* was holding up well, but stress, hunger and thirst were taking their silent toll on the trio.

Without warning, Dimple Sue stopped, loosened the pig's front legs from beneath Quaid's belt still anchoring it to the suitcase and rolled the porky orb onto the packed dirt road. With another involuntary, but irritating expulsion, the pig landed on its side. He was not destined to remain there for long. With a swift, energetic and well placed kick, Dimple Sue brought the pig back into the game and onto its stubby feet.

The morning sky, beautiful and dry showed the horizon from any angle. This clarity, combined with Quaid's height allowed him spy a small dust cloud grow increasingly larger as it appeared out of the horizon. Within a few minutes, a rusted stake truck loaded with a dozen hay bales approached the trio. The truck rolled to a stop with the predictable dust cloud in hot pursuit. After the dust cleared, the driver rolled down his window, tapped his hat brim and said, "Howdy-do."

Relieved to see another human being in this vast expanse both Quaid and Dimple Sue immediately replied with heartfelt Howdy-do's.

The truck driver, who gave his name as, Beedly Rackhorn, was like most country folk in West Texas, courteous but stoic. "Nice to meet cha'," Rackhorn said and almost smiled.

Beedly did not ask any uncomfortable questions regarding their circumstance and instead offered them water.

Quaid decided the best course of action was to tell only the necessary truths and wing the rest. He held out his hand, "Ed Bland's the name and this here is Miss Suzy Tibbs, my fiancée. Miss Tibbs instantly showed the appropriately distraught face of one who has lost much. Quaid explained, without much detail, that their pet pig had somehow ingested Miss Tibbs' engagement ring.

Beedly Rackhorn was empathetic to the couple's situation. He himself had once lost an engagement ring to a marauding raccoon after leaving it in the outhouse.

'Well," Rackhorn said, "not sure what do about this here sit-chi-ation, best we load ya'll into my truck and find us a veter-genarian see if he can hep' ya out."

It took all three individuals to heft the pig into the back of the truck; Quaid tossed the *Stryde Glider* on top of it. The undergarment gourmand continued to accept his circumstance and rolled comfortably against a bale of hay where he predictably fired off a companionable crepitation of startling magnitude.

"Sounds like in-di-gestion," Beedly commented, stepping upwind.

With very little conversation or fanfare, which was one of the things Quaid loved most about Texans, the three got in the truck and pulled away. Beedly offered them beef jerky and water which they gladly accepted. It had been a long few days and they were running on adrenalin vapors.

Unfortunately, Beedly had forgotten to re-install the tailgate. When he accelerated, the porker rolled out the back and hit the pavement at 20 miles an hour. Beedly screeched to a stop and a visibly distressed Dimple Sue stuffed the jerky into her mouth, climber over Quaid, jumped from the cab and ran toward the quivering livestock.

Pigs are just plain lucky, Quaid thought as he viewed the scene: because of its rotundness, the porker had managed to bounce and roll 50 feet rather than deliver a single oily fat-smear to the otherwise unblemished roadway.

The pig did not appear injured or overly concerned and slowly got to its feet shaking both its head and tail at the same time. Not sure what to do, Dimple Sue and Quaid looked at each other and then glanced around. There, not 10 feet back up the road, were the ingested panties, now freed by fortuitous impact and still embracing the lipstick bag.

The pig, Dimple Sue and Quaid were instantly and unanimously relieved. Quaid dashed to the small bundle, picked it up and instantly regretted doing so.

The stoic Rackhorn continued to show little emotion or interest and calmly walked to his truck to grab a bottle of water.

He returned and handed it to Quaid who doused the nasty parcel until it was fairly clean, (*You can't polish a turd, his dad used to say*) then walked back to the truck, un-wrapped it, hung Dimple Sue's black lace panties over the passenger side rear view mirror and stuffed the bag into his pocket.

Beedly glanced at the red bag stenciled REVLON, "I've heard of lipstick on a pig, but lipstick in a pig, that's a new one," he opinioned and frequently glanced at Dimple Sue's unmentionable drying on the mirror.

They reloaded the pig and motored on to a small truck stop less than 20 minutes away. Less than half a mile before they stopped, Quaid noticed a large, flat, hard packed field and in the distance a twin engine Beechcraft Bonanza A36 sitting alone near a wide metal shed.

Beedly Rackhorn slowed to a stop and looked at his passengers. "Here we is, folks," he said in a flat Texas drawl, as predictable and dry as trailing dust ball that engulfed them.

"Thanks for the ride, Mr. Beedly!" Dimple Sue said after the desert dandruff cleared and gave him a quick peck on the cheek.

"You betcha Miss Suzy Tibbs, you folks take care now ... Hey, hold on there a minute! What about the pig and the panties?"

"You keep the pig, we'll take the panties. Thanks again, partner!" Quaid smiled.

"No problem, makes sense to me, Mr. Bland. Give me your address and I'll send you some bacon."

"OINK!"

CHEAP THOUGHTS

"**A** penny for your thoughts, Quaid," Dimple Sue smiled. Her previously supple red lips were now the color of a mud flat and she was running a close second to Quaid and the porker in the smell category.

"Save your money, I'm not sure their worth it."

Quaid licked the dust off his lips and looked around. "This road trip stuff is getting old. I think it's time we change our modus and ride in style. Fluff up Miss Dimple Sue, we got work to do."

For most of his life Quaid, driven by the clarity adrenalin delivers, had been able to collate unfortunate circumstances into energy that usually propelled him out a shit storm His life was like squeezing a grapefruit seed, it pops out fast and no one knows where it's going.

It took 20 minutes to walk back to the dirt landing strip Quaid had noticed.

"Let's see if we can find the owner of that plane and maybe make a deal," Quaid suggested.

Dimple Sue fluffed as instructed. She said "I, for one, am all in."

What a girl, Quaid thought.

The large aircraft hanger was closed, but Quaid found a steel door on the side of the structure and thumped on it with what he considered a friendly series of thumps. It was quiet and then they heard a something heavy drop on the floor inside. "Aieee!"

Roper Begley, dressed in a wizards robe and flip flops, was not accustomed to unannounced or un-vetted visitors arriving at his secluded hanger. If he hadn't been concentrating on a project he would have seen them approaching on his 8-bank, HD video monitor array. Roper hesitated before heading towards the door. His space, his haven, was being invaded. This concern broke his concentration, causing Roper to knock a heavy spanner wrench off a work bench and onto his bare foot. Even through the grey steel door, Quaid and Dimple Sue could hear clearly.

"Aieee!! FUCK, fUck, fuCk, fucK, fuck...!"

"Guys," Dimple Sue said and smiled demurely, "is that all you think about?"

Quaid banged again and then tested the door handle. It opened easily and they peered inside to find a large open area with work benches and lockers lining the perimeter wall. The place was immaculate, painted all white like an operating room for whales. At the far end, two red aviation fuel tanks stood near the hanger door and in front of him was a tall man squatting on the floor holding his right foot. There was blood on the ground.

"Howdy," Quaid said in a harmless voice.

The man raised a bloody hand. His voice was hoarse from hurling expletives. "Howdy yer own damn self. Look what you gone an' made me do. You see me here, bleeding on the floor, well, that's yer doing. Whaddaya want? Make it quick before I take a notion to whack you with that damn spanner!"

"Well mister, we sure are sorry," Dimple Sue said with words and eyes. "Here, let me take a look at that foot."

Dimple Sue entered the hanger, walked towards the man and flashed *that* smile then leaned over and touched his foot. Well, that was that. The yelper stopped yelping, momentarily and took a closer look at dusty, busty Dimple Sue. This here's some woman, he said to himself between yelps, but she sure could use a bath.

Quaid smiled. He found himself liking this crazy Dimple Sue Pankersley more every day. Is this how love starts, he wondered. Circumstances had changed quickly lately and had been no time to absorb his evolving emotions. Hence, Quaid set his mind to work like a shrimp net. He caught good stuff as he trawled the ocean of time but always remembered to dump the by-catch.

After examining the man's foot, Dimple Sue asked for some disinfectant, bandages and tape. The man worked his way up and onto a nearby rollerball office chair then pushed himself over to a row of stainless steel cabinets. He appeared to be in pain and somewhat confused about his current situation. Perhaps it was this confusion that caused him to open the wrong locker. There were no first-aid supplies inside the 8 foot tall locker instead, backed by bright LED lights, it brimmed with conventional and unconventional weapons, all displayed in perfect oily arrangement. The bottom of locker housed dozens of boxes of ammunition, night vison goggles and specialized tools.

"Oops, wrong locker, sorry folks," the man said with no sign of embarrassment and closed the door, but not before noting Quaid's expression. He pushed further down the room and came to another locker which did have numerous first-aid items. Dimple Sue set about bandaging his foot while Quaid determined the best way to approach the situation.

ROPER

The man asked, "What brings you folks up this way? Looks like you might've had a long row to hoe." After another involuntary whiff of Dimple Sue, the man casually reached behind to turn on a fan and sprayed some nearby WD 40 in the air.

"Well, it's a bit of a story," Quaid said, "Not very interesting, but let's just say we arrived here by fortuitous circumstance."

"Well, you're right, that's not very interesting, so cut the crap young fella. I can see you're up to something, I can smell it, (along with a pig,) something weird and therefore something exciting is going on and it just so happens I love weird and fexciting. I can afford it too."

Roper grimaced and eyeballed Quaid as Dimple Sue put the final wraps on his foot. "I saw you eyeballing my guns. You familiar with modern armaments, Mr...?"

"Sorry partner, we should have introduced ourselves earlier, it's just when I see blood I sometimes forget my manners. I'm Quaid and this is Miss Dimple Sue. Quaid knew he could not keep up a charade and still make his hope for a plan work.

"Nice to meet you," Dimple Sue said as she stood up and stretched. "Feeling better?"

"Ahhhhhhh ..." Roper was mesmerized.

Dimple Sue snapped her fingers to pull the man of out his double deep eyeball dive.

"Ah, oh yes, nice to meet you folks as well. The man held up a bloody hand and settled for a fist bump. "I'm Roper Begley, us Begley's been in Oklahoma for three generations. We own some oil wells around here, my granddaddy got hold of some parcels over ninety years ago in a land trade with the local Kickapoo Indians. My wife's name is Clawdeen Pancake. She's all Kickapoo, I'll tell ya that."

Dimple asked, "Is she here?"

"Nope, she's outback feeding her beavers. Don't know why she keeps them dam things around, tradition maybe, but they stinks worse than a skunk and that constant slappin' and flappin' can turn man cold inside, I'll tell you that. Tried to make a hat out of one, but little mud beater wouldn't sit still, scratched my head all up, I'll tell ya."

Before closing the cabinet door, Roper reached behind a large bottle of iodine and pulled out a fifth of Johnny Walker Red.

"Little something to ease the pain, White Man's medicine, I'll tell ya." he said and tipped the bottle towards Quaid and Dimple Sue.

"Don't mind if we do," Quaid said followed by Dimples Sue's eager nodding's.

It *had* been a long row to hoe and now, if they played their cards right, Quaid hoped they could escape the "curse of the stones" and get on with a relationship that seemed well-worth pursuing.

"Time," Roper said after half the bottle had been evacuated, "is not what it used to be. Time is my currency now and I intend to ride the time bomb of life," he looked with inebriated appreciation at his Rolex Oyster, "as long as I can, just like Ol' Slim Pickens done Doctor Strangelove, Tic, tic...tic..."

It was a sober situation, with only drunks in attendance.

By now Quaid's only concern was the obvious evaporation taking place in the Johnny Walker bottle and somehow it seemed the right time to broach what Quaid hoped would be a mutually beneficial arrangement.

Before Quaid could begin, Roper reached behind him and pulled a Martin D4 guitar from the top of a wall locker and without further comment he began:

> *"Son, I've made a life*
> *out of readin' people's faces*
> *knowin' what the cards were*
> *by the way they held their eyes*
> *so if you don't mind me sayin'*
> *I can see you're out of aces*
> *for a taste of your whiskey*
> *I'll give you some advice"*

"Nice, Kenny Rogers, right?" Dimple Sue remarked and handed Roper the bottle, who then took down its last swallow, then he pulled a fatty out and asked Quaid for a light and the nightly got deathly quie...Wait a minute, Quaid thought, is this normal. One toke later he knew the answer. He was both tired and relieved.

Quaid started by telling Roper the truth. It felt odd, but was necessary if they were to get any further with a plan.

It was not surprising that Roper was most interested in the emerald part of the story and appeared to understand the problem and the complications involved.

"So, if I've got this right," Roper said, " You two are sitting on a bag of emeralds that have at least two deaths attached to them and are being hunted by of a band of unsavory characters?"

"Yup, that pretty well sums it up." Dimple Sue nodded.

"It also sounds to me," Roper went on, like ya'll need to get back to Key West so you don't dehydrate and dry up over worrying about this."

Quaid liked like this kind of talk, even though he knew it was usually bullshit.

"That's right, Mr. Roper, I need to get back work doing what I know how to do."

"Yeah," Dimple Sue said, "I miss my life there, too. You got any ideas cowboy?"

"Well, funny you should ask, here's the way I see it, I've got a plane and I've got money, I've got a fort, a gun or two and a hankering for a little fun. What I suggest we do is, you give me those emeralds and I'll fly you to Key West and spot you two thousand dollars to get settled. For your part, you will contact the Miami ass-wipes and give them my name, address and phone number. I'll take it from there." Hic! Hic!

Without seeming to understand what was happening, Roper set into a series of high-pitched hiccups. He looked surprised every time an involuntary spasm burst forth.

"I, Hic! never had, Hic! this hap, Hic! Befo... HIC!

This went on for a few minutes. Dimple Sue and Quaid quickly offered numerous common remedies; hold your breath, drink water upside down, stick your fingers in your nose, stop breathing and other absurd remedies. However, out of a sense of courtesy, Roper tried several cures without success and soon Quaid began to worry about Ropers health. The guy was taking a good whuppin,' that's for sure.

After a brief, sympathetic shrug, Dimple Sue sighed, she looked bored and sleepy. She stood, stretched and walked around distractedly, and in the process silently eased up behind Roper.

"Hic, hic ...!" Roper appeared to be fighting for his life. Bad way to go, Quaid thought.

Dimple pulled her .38 and placed it firmly against the back of Ropers head. She cocked the revolver and pulled the trigger-CLICK! It rhymed with HIC, Dimple Sue noted. To avoid an accident, she'd unloaded her gun earlier.

'What the fuh! ... Hold on, hold on, 1,2,3 ... Their Gone!" Roper said without interruption. "Miss Dimple Sue, you got a mighty fine style about you, darlin'. Let's do some bidness."

After a few generous servings of conversation, Johnny Red and a handshake to seal the deal, Roper set up two cots and left the hanger with a, "Holler if you need me!"

The day became dimmer, the situation clear and a sense of excitement began to spread. Nearby, a high plains coyote howled harmony to the wailing tires on a passing cattle truck.

Talked out and tired, they fell asleep holding hands across an empty space, silently admiring each other's ability to find humor in almost any situation, so far. Still, for both, a return to Key West was essential.

Both knew that to free oneself from being hunted, one must become the hunter.

FIN

"Fair Winds and Following Seas ..."
To all who held the literary rabbit for me to chase.
The *Ladies of the Pen* – Robin Robinson, Carol Lazar and Toby Armour.
Publisher and confidant – Shirrel Rhoades and his faithful Indian companion, Chuck Newman.
The Mystical Proofer – Kathy Russ.
A generous man with his hard earned knowledge – Michael Haskins.
Artist on a High Wire – JT Thompson.
Inspiration and man of mystery – Jim Linder.
John and Vicki Hanson – Nomads of the art world.
And finally,
The Committee who refused to read one word until the story was complete and remains resistant to this day.
Love y' all ... it was great fun.

Key West, 2016

ABOUT THE AUTHOR

Captain Mark T. "Reef" Perkins is a marine surveyor with a colorful past. From commanding a 150-foot 300 DWT US Army diving ship off Vietnam to smuggling in the Caribbean, Reef Perkins has become a living legend. A graduate of both the US Army Engineer Officer Candidate School and the US Navy Salvage Officers School, he's a man comfortable in or out of the water. Raised in rural Michigan, Reef now lives in Key West where he can get his feet wet. He is the author of the bestselling memoir, *Sex, Salvage & Secrets*, and the humorous short story collection, *Screwed, Blu'd and Tattooed*.

Thank you for reading.
Please review this book. Reviews
help others find Absolutely Amazing eBooks and
inspire us to keep providing these marvelous tales.
If you would like to be put on our email list
to receive updates on new releases,
contests, and promotions, please go to
AbsolutelyAmazingEbooks.com and sign up.

AbsolutelyAmazingEbooks.com
or AA-eBooks.com

For sales, editorial information, subsidiary rights information
or a catalog, please write or phone or e-mail

AbsolutelyAmazingEbooks
Manhanset House
Shelter Island Hts., New York 11965, US
Tel: 212-427-7139
www.BrickTowerPress.com
bricktower@aol.com
www.IngramContent.com

For sales in the UK and Europe please contact our distributor,
Gazelle Book Services
White Cross Mills
Lancaster, LA1 4XS, UK
Tel: (01524) 68765 Fax: (01524) 63232
email: jacky@gazellebooks.co.uk